INFERNO OF LOVE

A STAR-CROSSED LOVERS FIREMAN ROMANCE

FIREFIGHTERS OF LONG VALLEY ROMANCE
BOOK TWO

ERIN WRIGHT

To Handsome Hubby:
Thanks for being willing to walk through fire to save me, even if it's
just my attempt to cook dinner that set the kitchen ablaze.

CHAPTER 1

GEORGIA

APRIL, 2018

TRIPP POPPED HIS HEAD around her office door even as he gave a light rap on it. "Hey Georgia, there's a handsome cowboy here to see you."

"Thanks," Georgia Rowland said lightly, trying to ignore the warning bells going off in her head. If it was Levi, this was going to become real awkward, real quick. Not that Levi exactly came strolling into her office every day, but it was possible that he—

And then Moose came striding in instead. Georgia's stomach did the amazing trick of both dropping to somewhere around her knee caps, while also rising up in her throat. She was going to be the first human on record with a bifurcated stomach.

Awesome.

Moose. Of course it was Moose. Someone she'd known since they were in diapers, someone she'd graduated with from high school, and…the one guy she'd always wanted but could never have.

He was here to torture her with his cologne and muscular chest and mmhmmm thighs and…

"How are you?" she asked, planting a bright smile on her lips. She came around her desk to do the awkward hug/handshake combo that always left her feeling like she needed to bust out with, "And that's what it's all about!" when she was done.

Except she was the youngest branch manager in the history of the Goldfork Credit Union, and a female to boot. Busting out with the lyrics from the *Hokey Pokey* in her office (or anywhere, really) was not going to happen any time soon.

It was easy enough to stay professional and distant from older, crusty farmers who'd been tilling up the land since Moses came down from Mt. Sinai with his arms full of stone tablets. It was slightly harder to keep that demeanor up around Moose.

He flashed a mouth full of gorgeous, straight white teeth at her and said, "Good, good, but if the farmers don't quit bitching about the water year that's in the cards, I think I just might lose my ever-lovin' mind."

"I've been hearing that around town," Georgia murmured, but left it at that. She wasn't about to get into the politics of lending to farmers in what was projected to be a low-water year, not even with Moose.

"Well anyway, I don't know if you've heard that the spaghetti feed and donkey basketball fundraiser is coming up quick, but the fire department is sending all of us out into the community to ask for donations to auction off. Do you have anything to add to the pile?"

"Oh. Hmmm…" She tapped her forefinger against her teeth as she thought. As the branch manager for the only credit union in Sawyer, she got asked quite often for donations and prizes for local fundraisers, so they had their stack of branded t-shirts, pens, and notepads that they gave to anyone who asked. But with Moose giving her the "I'd love you forever if you gave me something great" look, it was hard to brush him off with a pile of Goldfork Credit Union t-shirts.

All right, so maybe he wasn't *actually* giving her that look, and she was just projecting her own feelings onto him. That was totally a possibility.

She decided that was a thought she didn't really want to explore any further.

"Oh hey!" she exclaimed suddenly when inspiration struck, "what if we match a $50 deposit into a savings account for anyone under the age of 18? Help a kid get started on saving for something important. Grandparents would love to give a gift like that to a grandchild."

He sent her a huge smile, his eyes crinkling in the corners with happiness. Her stomach dropped further, hitting right around her shin bones or so, while simultaneously strangling her by rising further in her throat.

This was starting to get ridiculous, really.

"I love it!" Moose said enthusiastically, completely oblivious to what he was doing to her insides. "Do you need to pass it by headquarters?"

"Nah, they give us some money every year to do community-minded stuff like this," Georgia said, waving a hand dismissively, trying to act casual, as if chitchatting with Moose was no big deal. "If, uh, we end the year with money in that account, we get a talkin' to about not donating enough to the local groups. Of course, that's a pretty rare thing – usually we're asked for more than we have the money for."

He chuckled. "Yeah, Dad has the same thing happen, but he usually just gives away John Deere toys to auction off when he's asked for donations."

"'Just'?" she echoed, one eyebrow raised. "I've seen the price tags on those toys. They don't come cheap!"

"Nothing John Deere does comes cheap," Moose agreed with a grin. "Quality all the way." He flexed his muscles like a bodybuilder for a moment, and Georgia burst out laughing.

"I forget sometimes that your actual name is Deere," she

said dryly. "Your father is one dedicated John Deere dealership owner, you know that?"

"I'm pretty sure I know that better than anyone else alive," he said, and there was something in his eyes for just a moment and then it was gone, his grin firmly planted on his face again. "Ever since I was a kid, I've wondered what I'll name my oldest son. John, Deere the Second, or Green are pretty much my only choices."

"'Green'?" she repeated, laughing. "You'd name a child 'Green'?!"

"Hell, my father named me Deere. I'm pretty sure all naming conventions are thrown out the window at this point."

"True enough." They grinned at each other for a moment, and Georgia felt a flash of desire roar through her veins as the stomach flipping resumed.

Okay, this was *really* getting out of control.

Her brain knew, even if her stomach didn't, that Moose Garrett was off-limits. He was so far off-limits, he might as well have a "No Trespassing" sign stapled to his forehead. In fact, she might just donate one to the cause, to help her stomach remember this information. Someday, when Moose was ready to settle down and pop out boys named Green, he was going to be doing it with Tennessee, Georgia's cousin.

And nice human beings simply didn't daydream about stealing their cousin's future fiancé, that was for damn sure.

"Well, I best get a move on," Moose said, shifting from one foot to the other. He was constantly on the move, even when he was standing still. Georgia figured that must be how he stayed in such good shape, even as their former high school classmates were starting to develop spare tires around the middle. "I just stopped by to do a deposit and thought I'd check in with you on the prize thing while I was here. Would you mind getting the info over to Jaxson? This is his first fundraiser for the fire department, and he's more nervous than a long-tailed cat in a room full of rocking chairs. Honestly," he said confidentially, his voice dropping a little as if to keep from being overheard, "I don't think taking care of Sugar after the Muffin Man fire has helped anything."

"Yeah, I can see that," Georgia said, nodding slowly. The new fire chief'd had to save his girlfriend from a fire down at the local bakery, and Georgia figured that was enough to make anyone a bit overwrought. "I kept meaning to bring a casserole by and see how Sugar's doing. I heard she's mostly got her voice back – is that true?"

A smart-ass grin spread across Moose's face. "Jaxson's been telling me that it's come back just in time for her to start harping on him about how she isn't an invalid, and that he needs to go back to work and leave her the hell alone."

Georgia let out a snort of laughter at that. She didn't know the new fire chief all that well – he'd only started in January – but she did know Sugar, and that sounded just like her. She was a pretty independent person, and if Jaxson was prone to hovering…well, Sugar probably wouldn't take that real well.

"I'm glad that she's at least feeling good enough to tell him to back off," Georgia said with a grin. "I'm pretty sure that's a good sign, and if he's smart, he'll listen to her."

"Smart men listen to the women in their lives," Moose agreed, "at least if they know what's good for 'em."

He was looking at her a little *too* intently, and Georgia felt her cheeks flush under his gaze. It was…awkward. And weird. She coughed, then coughed again. Then cleared her throat. Because apparently a whole slew of frogs had taken up residence in it.

"I'm sure Tennessee would be happy to hear that," she finally said weakly.

"Right. Tennessee." And then he was walking towards the door. "Thanks for your help," he tossed over his shoulder as he slipped through and her office door shut with a *click* behind him and she was left just staring at it.

"Yeah. Anytime," she whispered into the quiet of her office.

Somehow, she'd messed that up and she didn't even know how…but she did know she regretted it.

Even if she shouldn't.

CHAPTER 2
MOOSE

MOOSE PUSHED HIS WAY to the bar at O'Malley's and flagged down Steve, the owner and full-time bartender. "Guinness," he shouted over the twang of country music. Steve jerked his head in response, pulled a dark brown bottle out from underneath the counter, and popped the top even as he was sliding it towards Moose.

A body didn't own a bar for 25 years without getting some movements down to a smooth ballet, that was for damn sure.

Moose dropped four singles on the bar top and then turned to lean up against it, sipping his beer while looking around the darkened bar. It was a Friday night, and it showed. Lots of people out on the town, ready to let their hair down and have some fun.

Levi was supposed to show up any minute now. Moose would nurse his beer along; Levi would buy him a second one over Moose's protestations; and they'd both ignore the fact that the heir to the richest guy in town was poorer than a church mouse.

So, you know, the usual.

Levi seemed to be taking his sweet-ass time about making his appearance this week, though, so Moose just settled into place against the polished bar top and slowly sipped at his beer. Several of the biggest customers of the Garrett Tractor & Implement Dealership were here tonight, which was both a blessing and a curse. Any face-time with customers outside of work, where they got to see him as more than just a salesman trying to upgrade them to the latest and greatest, was always a good thing.

Of course, his father letting him back onto the sales floor was only something Moose could wish for longingly at this point. He'd been stuck in the repair shop for a lot longer than he'd expected and was ready to move back to the showroom, where his natural talent for salesmanship could truly be a boon to the business.

He understood why his dad was having him work in every department at the dealership – as the future owner, having a deep knowledge of how everything worked together was key – but he was never going to truly love being a grease monkey. The sales floor was where he shined, and everyone knew it.

But tonight, here at the bar, he was the owner's son, even if he was the son tucked away in the repair shop, and the dealership's biggest, most important customers would expect him to buy a round or two for them, which…wasn't necessarily doable. He did some mental calculations. If he bought a beer for three farmers, what would that mean for paying his cell phone bill next week? Could he squeak by until payday?

"Hey, brother," Levi said in his ear. Moose jumped, spilling a little of his Guinness on the scuffed wooden floor.

"Shit, Levi," Moose yelped, laughing and swiping at the stray beer that'd splattered on his shirt. "When'd you get here?"

"Just now, but you seemed off in your own little world. Trying to figure out who you can afford to buy rounds for?"

"Maybe," Moose said with a shrug, settling back against the bar top. He took another tiny sip of his beer. The smaller, the better. He'd taken nursing a beer to an Olympic level, really.

"You know I'd be happy to pay for the rounds," Levi

rumbled. His deep voice didn't travel far, but Moose'd had 17 years of practice listening to him, so he caught every word.

"It'll be fine," Moose said, waving the suggestion off. Customers expected the owner's son to buy their drinks, not the dealership's welder and repairman. "How was work today? I didn't see you at closing time."

"Your dad has me out doing repairs in the fields right now. That damn wind today was colder than an ice slick in January, though. I'll be glad when spring repairs are over with, and I can come back to working in the shop."

Levi worked at the John Deere dealership too, of course, although he made more money there than Moose did. *Everyone* made more money than Moose did.

In fact, Moose was pretty damn sure that the shop kid who just started last week and did nothing more than push a broom around made more than he did.

He pushed the thought aside. "Are all of the farmers complaining to you about how dry it is this year? That's all I'm hearing about right now at the dealership."

"Yup. This past winter…I mean, sure, we had a few nice snowstorms but half the time, we were getting nothing but wind blowing the same damn snow around in circles. The snowpack up in the Goldfork Mountains just isn't where it should be…I don't know. I guess we'll see. If we get a few late season storms in, we might be fine, but right now, all we're getting is wind, wind, and more wind. Like living in a damn air tunnel. Drying out the fields like this ain't exactly making the farmers happy."

Moose took another metered sip of his beer. "Nope, it really isn't. And if the farmers ain't happy…"

"Ain't nobody happy," Levi finished, and they laughed. They lapsed together into a silence that felt as natural and comfortable as slipping on an old pair of jeans. Levi was his oldest and truest friend; the one who'd always had his back no matter what.

Moose may have a dick for a father, but Levi almost helped make up for that.

Almost.

Of course, Levi's dad was no one to write home about either, although he was a dirtbag in a completely different way. While Moose's dad was the richest guy in town and someone no one dared stand up to, Levi's dad was the town drunk who didn't care one bit about who or what he hurt, as long as he got alcohol in the end.

They didn't appear similar on the surface, but underneath…

Neither one cared about anyone but themselves. Neither one even cared about their own sons.

Dickwads, the lot of 'em.

"What did your dad say when you told him you wouldn't be bringing brown paper bags by anymore?" Moose asked, taking another tiny sip of his Guinness. Despite his best efforts, his beer was almost gone. Maybe he could pretend to drink out of an empty bottle; extend the illusion a little longer.

He was good at pretending.

Levi shrugged, looking out at the dance floor where a few rowdy cowboys were staggering to the beat of their own drum, since it obviously wasn't to the beat of the country music thumping through the speakers. "Eh. He questioned my parentage. Told me not to come back. You know, the usual."

Moose nodded. It *was* the usual. That didn't mean it hurt any less, though.

"You think he's ready to go to some meetings yet?"

"Nope." Levi popped the "p" for extra emphasis, and then gave Moose a wry smile. "I reckon he'll be ready for that about the same time I'm ready to strip down to my boxers and run down Main Street."

Moose nodded again. Levi was right, of course. His dad was nowhere near ready to give up the bottle. Maybe someday he would be.

Today was not that day.

Hours later, Moose let himself into the basement entrance to his parents' house and down to his bedroom, where he unlaced his boots and settled back on the bed with a huge sigh. He'd gotten away with only having to buy two beers for customers tonight, which he figured was some sort of win. People probably wondered why he still lived at home; why he drove a beat-up truck; why he nursed the same beer for hours at a time down at the bar. He imagined the guesses ranged from he was a tightwad through to him being a lightweight with alcohol.

He didn't imagine that the guesses were ever on the money, though (all puns intended) – that his father was hellbent on "toughening up his son" by paying him pauper's wages down at the dealership. When Moose finally got to take over the business, he'd be rolling in the dough, but until then, he was the poorest rich kid this side of the Mississippi. It was something he'd told only Levi, and only because it *was* Levi.

Moose just had to make it through five more years of hell, and then it would all be his. He could totally do it.

Totally.

CHAPTER 3
GEORGIA

THE SILVERWARE CLINKED in the awkward silence that was the Rowland Sunday Dinner.

Just because it happened every single week didn't make it any less awkward. Unfortunately.

This week was at Uncle Robert and Aunt Roberta's house, which meant they were eating on matching china plates with real silver and sipping $300-a-bottle wine out of delicate goblets.

It was exactly the kind of thing that made Georgia grateful that she was the daughter to the *younger* of the Rowland brothers – the one who'd inherited nothing at all and was now a high school biology teacher – because if she had to eat off real china using real silver every day, she'd probably be stark-raving mad by now.

Uncle Robert cleared his throat and looked pointedly at Tennessee. "What did your piano teacher assign to you this week?" he asked. "I haven't heard you practice lately."

Which was code for, "In the last ten minutes."

Georgia sliced off a small bite of her roast beef and popped it in her mouth as she waited for her gorgeous and super talented cousin to respond to her father's probing.

Actually, she realized as she chewed the tender meat, eating off china and silver wasn't such a bad thing, really. It was having Robert Rowland as a father that would do her in.

Tennessee took a small sip of her moscato. "He has me working on some Vivaldi pieces right now," she said with a polite smile at her dad. She was as poised and gracious as ever. As far as Georgia could tell, Tennessee never got rattled, not about anything at all. "And I practiced earlier today," she continued smoothly. "Perhaps you were outside and didn't hear me."

Virginia, Tenny's younger sister, jumped into the fray, but whether it was to give a reprieve to her older sister for a moment or because she was dying for some attention herself, Georgia couldn't tell. She never knew with Virginia. "Did you hear, Father?" she asked eagerly. "My cello instructor said that if I keep it up, I might get into Juilliard next year, after I graduate. He said—"

"That's nice, darlin'," Aunt Roberta cut her off coldly, "but we were talking about your sister's musical career." She gave Virginia a pointed look, who promptly slunk down in her seat.

"Yes, Momma," she said into her goblet of ice water.

"And stop slouching."

Virginia obediently sat up.

Georgia kept a stiff smile on her lips as she cut into her potato. She could feel her mom practically vibrating with anger to her left, but she too said nothing. It would only cause problems to try to point out to Robert and Roberta that their younger daughter had potential too; problems for everyone involved. They'd take it out on Georgia and her parents, sure, but they'd take it out even more on Virginia. It wouldn't be kind to the teenager to stand up for her, as much as that reality sucked ass.

"Has Deere asked you to attend the fire department fundraiser with him?" Uncle Robert asked Tennessee, ignoring his younger daughter's comment completely.

Georgia swallowed, hard, and a small piece of potato went down the wrong tube. She started coughing politely into her hand, desperately trying to pretend that everything was fine, but she soon gave into a full-body cough, huddled over in her chair, tears streaming down her face from the force of the coughing.

Her mom patted her on the back. "Are you okay, dear?" she murmured as Georgia struggled for air. Her face was hot with embarrassment, but *finally* the coughing fit passed, the potato unlodged itself from her airway, and she was able to breathe without lapsing into another coughing fit.

"So sorry," she murmured into her goblet of moscato. "Eating sure is dangerous sometimes."

No one laughed.

"He hasn't yet," Tennessee said, politely answering her father's question as if nothing had happened. She gave a small shrug. "We might just meet there. Honestly, Father, I don't think he's ready—"

"Of course he is; he just doesn't know it yet," her father snapped. "He's a typical male, is all. But his dad and I have talked, and it's settled. As soon as Deere is ready, he'll propose. His dad has made it *quite* clear that he doesn't get the dealership until then, so I imagine he'll be ready soon. His dad has him working as a grease monkey right now, helping with oil changes in the shop, and he certainly won't want *that* job for long. He's going to want to take things over, and he knows that marriage to you is how that'll happen."

Tenny nodded, her curled and styled hair falling forward to cover her face. "Of course," she murmured into her dinner plate.

So yeah, maybe being the daughter of the high school biology teacher wasn't such a bad thing after all. The principal didn't demand that Georgia marry someone who would take over the English department; no one really cared who she married, honestly, as long as he was a vaguely decent guy. Her parents wouldn't exactly get behind a pothead or a thief, but they also didn't sit around the dinner table and grill her about her marriage prospects.

Thank God for small favors.

She shot a grateful smile at her parents, sitting side by side, politely working their way through the beautifully cooked food. After this week's torture was over, her mother would happily throw on a pair of sweatpants, put her hair up in a ponytail, and get to work on her oil paintings. Her dad would put on his work jeans and go putter around in the garage; probably work on the lawn mower that'd been giving him fits. Get it ready for the upcoming season.

And Georgia would head back to her condo, home to her and her two goldfish, and read a book while curled up in bed.

It wasn't an exciting life, but it was *theirs*, and compared to the rich branch of the family, Georgia couldn't help but be grateful for it. If money turned a person into Uncle Robert and Aunt Roberta, she figured being middle class for the rest of her life was something she'd be happy with.

The topic of conversation turned to water – not enough of it, as always – and the wind – which was busy drying everything out like a nature-sized hair dryer – and Tennessee, grateful to have the spotlight off her for the moment, began picking at her food with a little more enthusiasm.

Another week, another Sunday dinner.

Georgia suddenly had visions of spending Sunday afternoon with her aunt and uncle when she was 72, the conversation just as stilted and awkward as it was now. A half century of Sunday dinners would do nothing to bring them closer together as a family.

And then the idea of Moose sitting next to Tennessee entered into the daydream, and Georgia felt her heart squeeze at the thought. Someday, Tenny was going to marry Moose, and she'd probably want Georgia as her maid of honor, and Georgia would have to pretend to be happy even as her heart was being stomped to pieces…

"Are you okay?" Virginia's voice broke into her thoughts, and Georgia's head jerked up.

"Yes, of course," she murmured, taking another sip of her moscato.

She was good at pretending.

She had to be.

CHAPTER 4

MOOSE

"**S**IX DAYS LEFT, GUYS," Jaxson said, pushing his fingers through his dark brown hair. He had bags under his eyes and clearly hadn't shaved for a couple of days.

He looked like a guy at the end of his rope, in other words.

"What's left to figure out?" he asked the room as a whole. "Did everyone go talk to their assigned local businesses?"

"I talked to everyone on my list," Moose said, "plus I chatted with Georgia over at the credit union."

He felt Levi stiffen up next to him. "*I* was supposed to talk to Georgia," he practically growled.

Moose lifted an eyebrow of surprise at his best friend's surliness. "I was there making a deposit, and saw that her office was empty. I figured why not chat with her while I had the chance, right?"

"Whatever," Levi mumbled, clicking his ballpoint pen rapidly as he stared down at the scarred tabletop. "What is she donating?"

"Ummm...bank deposits for kids," Moose said, a little more cautiously. "If a parent or grandparent puts $50 into a child's account, the bank will match it. She thought it'd be a good way to encourage children to save for college or whatever."

"She's already swung by here and filled out the paperwork for it," Jaxson put in, oblivious to the sudden tension between Levi and Moose. "She's on the done list. Luke, have you talked to Betty down at the diner yet?"

As the conversation shifted to less tension-fraught topics, Moose sighed to himself and tried to ignore Levi's pissed-off demeanor. If he reacted like this simply because Moose had talked to Georgia, what would he do if Moose *kissed* Georgia?

Not, of course, that Moose would do that. He was going to marry Tennessee. Everything was practically settled except for the ring and a date. Her father wanted it, his father wanted it, Tennessee wanted it, and Moose wanted it.

Okay, so all of that was true except for the last part. "Want" was a strong word, honestly. Moose had…resigned himself to it. Marrying Tennessee was what he was supposed to do, and Moose always did what he was supposed to do.

As…uninspiring as Moose's love life was, though, at least it wasn't a disaster zone like Levi's. Levi and Georgia had dated for three years, starting in high school and going through to the end of their first year in college, and their break-up hadn't exactly been stellar, unfortunately. Since then, from all outward appearances, Georgia had moved on and was fine with her life.

Levi, meanwhile, was stuck deeper than a 4x4 buried up to its axle in mud.

Oh, he'd say that he'd moved on if anyone asked him, but Moose knew that was a lie, even if Levi didn't. His reaction tonight just proved it. Moose hadn't meant to step on Levi's toes by chatting with Georgia about the fundraiser but in retrospect, it should've been obvious that this was how it would go down.

With a start, he realized how awkward his wedding to Tennessee was going to be. Levi would be his best man, of course, and Georgia would be Tenny's maid of honor, obviously, which meant that Levi would be escorting Georgia down the aisle at the wedding. Levi and Georgia would be paired up throughout the whole affair. Levi would be loving every minute of it while Georgia…

Well, Georgia might reconsider their relationship and could even end up together with Levi by the end of it. Wouldn't that be good?

It would be good. Great, in fact. Back to old times – he and Tennessee; Georgia and Levi.

Nothing better.

Nothing at all.

CHAPTER 5
GEORGIA

S HE GOT OUT of her sedan and hurried across the blacktop to the high school gymnasium. Tripp should be here any minute now…she scanned the crowds headed into the basketball gym, hoping to catch sight of her assistant manager among the crush.

There he was. Leaning up against one of the columns outside of the row of doors leading into the gym, he already looked bored out of his skull. Attending social events to represent the credit union to the community wasn't exactly Tripp's strong suit. She'd tried to tell him that this was going to hurt his career long-term – the credit union president liked to see his employees out schmoozing with the locals – but…

Well, Tripp was Tripp. Trying to get him to change his mind on something was akin to trying to push a granite boulder up the side of the Tetons. He wasn't going to budge, and you'd do nothing but wear yourself out trying. It really was a damn good thing he was such a good-lookin' guy, and a lot of fun to be around. It helped when it came to forgiving him for his faults.

"Having fun?" she asked him with a straight face as he fell into step beside her.

"Loads." The sarcasm was so thick, she had visions of scraping it off with a butter knife.

"Well, thanks for agreeing to come with me anyway," she said as he opened one of the sets of glass doors for her. "How is Porky handling the strain of being left alone for the night?"

"She didn't even have the decency to look disgruntled," Tripp said with a disgruntled sigh. Georgia bit back her grin. "I fed her her evening can of dog food, and then she was off to sleep again. It's like she only cares about me because I am her source of food."

Georgia had to bite down on her lower lip even harder. Porky wasn't exactly the most energetic dog on the face of the planet, and she rather figured that this was *exactly* how Porky viewed Tripp, and every other human out there.

Before she could flip him shit about keeping his dog on a diet, the crowds were upon them and she had to get to work. There were community members aplenty to chat with and kids to hand lollipops to.

She glad-handed long-time customers of the credit union as she and Tripp wandered together around the silent auction area, checking out the donated items and the prices they were going for. Between discussions of planned weddings and birth announcements and the occasional complaint about a bank policy, Georgia scanned for items that hadn't had a bid registered for them yet.

She had a soft spot for donated items that weren't generating any interest, so she made sure to put down a couple of generous bids for otherwise ignored items. She wasn't exactly sure what she'd do with an owl clock whose eyes ticked back and forth with every swing of the pendulum, but she'd figure something out.

Maybe, she brightened with the thought, she could donate it to the senior citizen's center. Or better yet, she contemplated as she tapped her teeth with her forefinger, she could give it to someone who was blind. After all, only a blind person would appreciate its aesthetics…

Georgia wasn't the only one working the crowd tonight, she noted as she wandered away from the owl clock and down the table to look at hand-crotched washcloths, Tripp dogging her heels, muttering under his breath with every step. Jaxson and Troy from the fire department were mixing and mingling too, but they were doing it with firemen boots in hand, selling raffle tickets for a set of kayaks donated by the local river club.

She was impressed to see Jaxson chatting people up and moving around the gym with ease. If she didn't know any better, she would've guessed that he'd been in town all his life, instead of just a handful of months. When he'd first moved to town, people had struggled to get used to the idea of a "foreigner" being in charge of their fire department, but after he saved Sugar and Gage from the bakery fire…Well, people seemed to be singing a different tune. It was nice to see him fitting in so well.

Troy, on the other hand…he looked like he was in pain as he drifted around with the boot in hand, trying to pretend that he was enjoying himself. Georgia wondered for a minute who thought it was a good idea to put him in charge of schmoozing local residents. She'd known him practically all her life, and hadn't heard more than a couple dozen words from him in all that time. He made a brick wall seem downright talkative.

"C'mon," she said, grabbing Tripp's arm and pulling him towards Troy. "I want to buy some raffle tickets."

Tripp grumbled under his breath but followed along obediently behind her. Georgia ignored his protestations. At this point, he'd complain about a bikini-clad girl serving him a meal on a platter. He was bound and determined to be grumpy, and there wasn't a damn thing she or anyone else could do about it.

It was one of the reasons why their relationship worked so

well – she didn't try to change him, and he didn't pretend to give a damn.

"Hi, Troy," she said with a cheerful smile, looking up at the blond man in front of her. He was handsome, as long as you went for the scruffy, blond, silent type. If Georgia ever saw some woman manage to get Troy to say more than three words in a row to her, Georgia'd know it was true love. "How much are the tickets this year?"

"Five for six," he rumbled as he looked down at her intently. He had these gorgeous green eyes that she'd somehow never noticed before.

It really was too bad that the tall, silent, brooding guys just weren't her style because objectively, even she could tell that Troy was handsome enough to grace the cover of a firefighter magazine.

"I've got a ten," she said, rummaging through her purse and pulling the ten-dollar bill out triumphantly. He peeled twelve raffle tickets off the massive roll he'd been carrying around. Georgia looked at the roll with a laugh. "Y'all sure are an optimistic group," she said dryly. There were probably a thousand tickets on the roll. Just how many raffle tickets did they think they'd sell tonight?

Troy just shrugged and smiled.

"Where do I put your half?" she asked, busily separating the duplicate tickets from each other. One numbered ticket would go into the prize drawing; the matching other half would go into her purse as proof in case she actually won.

"Ummm…" Troy said, and then turned to point at a large glass bowl up at the front of the gym.

"Thanks!" she said, and headed off to put half of the tickets into the bowl, Tripp trailing along behind her.

"Troy does speak, right? Not just grunts and shrugs, but real honest-to-God words?" Tripp asked no one in particular as they made their way across the gym.

"Only when he has to," Georgia said with a shrug. "Not everyone is as loquacious as you."

Tripp ignored that jibe and looked around, probably hoping to find someone to flirt with. He'd played dutiful assistant manager for long enough; now it was time for him to go have some fun.

"I think the Stephenson girl is here tonight," Georgia said with a grin and a jerk of her head towards the blonde in question.

"Now we're talking," Tripp said with a cocky grin, and then he was gone, making his way across the crowded gym to do some flirting.

Georgia looked around with a heavy sigh. Even as snarky as he was being tonight, Tripp was still at least company. Without him to hang out with, she was going to be awkwardly by herself for the rest of the evening. Social events…they were the bane of her existence for this very reason. She didn't mind hanging out with the Long Valley community – not like Tripp did, anyway – but doing it by herself was starting to get old.

Old like me.

She pushed that thought away. She'd be 27 next year. It wasn't like she was hitting retirement age next week or something.

"What was that sigh for?" Levi asked at her elbow. She spun in a circle, her hand over her heart.

"Good Lord, I didn't hear you come up!" she said with a laugh. "How's it going so far?" She ignored the sigh question. Talking to Levi about how she felt lonely at these kinds of gatherings was *not* going to happen. He'd read something into that that plain wasn't there.

Nope, she wasn't gonna touch that with a ten-foot pole.

"Pretty good turnout so far. The donkeys are getting restless out back, so we'll probably have to round up the guys soon to start the basketball game."

Georgia smiled, happy to have something to discuss with

Levi that wasn't charged with awkward emotions. They could do friends. They could totally do friends. As long as Levi left any discussion of dating out of it, they'd be just fine.

"So, who's running this year's bet on the basketball game?" she asked, eager to continue the light, polite conversation.

"Mr. Leadbetter, although of course, I don't know that, and neither do you." He waggled his eyebrows with a grin. Betting money, even on something as innocuous as donkey basketball, wasn't technically permitted by Idaho state law.

It was a law everyone chose to overlook, even Sheriff Connelly, for at least one night a year.

She grinned back. "Who are you guys playing tonight?"

"A bunch of high school teachers and staff."

Georgia snorted with laughter at the idea of Mrs. Westingsmith riding a donkey around the gym while trying to huck a basketball at the hoop. Or even more insane…her father on the back of a donkey.

This was a game she wouldn't miss for the world.

"The odds are…definitely in our favor," Levi said, reading her snort of laughter correctly. "In the non-existent betting pool, of course."

"What betting pool?" Georgia asked innocently.

"Exactly."

"Who's running the betting pool this year?" Tennessee asked in Georgia's ear. Georgia spun on her heel to glare at her cousin. What was *up* with people sneaking up on her tonight?! She opened her mouth to yell at her or answer her question or… or…*something*, when she saw Moose standing right behind Tenny.

Her mouth went dry. He looked damned delectable tonight, there was no doubt about it. He was wearing slacks instead of jeans for once, and as good as she thought Wranglers looked on him, somehow slacks looked even better. Which should be illegal. His dress shirt – no tie – wasn't buttoned at the top, leaving a triangle of skin peeking out at her that she suddenly wanted to lick, just to see what it tasted like.

Her eyes jerked up to his, and she saw he was smiling slightly at her in greeting. He didn't seem to realize that she'd been undressing him with her eyes, and for that, she was eternally thankful. In the distance, she heard Levi begin to answer Tennessee's question and was vaguely grateful that they hadn't noticed her obsession with Moose's throat.

Shit, that made her sound like a damn vampire or something.

She tore her eyes away from the tempting spot – again – and up to his face. "Hi," she croaked. She cleared her throat and moved to his side so they were both facing Levi and Tenny, who were busy joking about whose job it was gonna be to clean up the donkey shit at the end of the night. Tenny's face looked positively radiant as she chatted with Levi, and the weight in Georgia's stomach just grew heavier. Of *course* she looked radiant. Her date was the cutest guy in five counties. Georgia would be ecstatic too if she were on Moose's arm tonight.

Which she wasn't. She totally wasn't, and she totally never would be, and she was totally fine with that.

Totally.

"Ready for the big game?" she asked Moose, trying to force her mind to focus on something other than what she absolutely could not have. "Going to do some stretches beforehand?"

Moose let out a belly laugh. "All I have to do is stay on a damn donkey and try to throw an orange ball through a big metal hoop. I don't think I need to do any stretches to warm up for this."

"Good point. I was just thinking about not placing an illegal bet on the game, but before I chose which side to absolutely not bet on, I was wondering – is the basketball coach on the teacher's team? Or is she skipping out tonight?" The high school basketball coach was five months pregnant, and didn't always have the energy needed to keep up with the teens, let alone do anything extra. Georgia wouldn't blame her for passing on the fundraiser.

"She's at home; I guess she had some pretty bad morning sickness all day today. Does that change your nonexistent bet?"

"I am sad to say that it does." She sent him a pitifully sad look and he let out a gust of laughter.

"Now hold on a good long minute, how long have you been friends with me? And even with all our years of friendship, you were willing to bet against me, and *for* your high school biology teacher?"

"Considering the high school biology teacher is my dad, yeah, probably. Although he didn't tell me that he'd be playing tonight. I wonder if he weaseled out of it somehow." Her dad wasn't exactly the kind of person who rode donkeys *or* played basketball regularly, let alone played basketball while riding a donkey. She would've been surprised to see him there, although it was for a good cause, so maybe. Stranger things had happened in the history of the universe.

Possibly.

"We should probably go chat with Jaxson and see when the game is going to be starting. The natives are getting restless," Levi interjected.

"Good idea. Ladies." Moose nodded to Georgia and Tennessee and then turned to walk away with Levi, two fantastic asses on display as they went.

"He has an ass you could bounce a quarter off," Tennessee said with a lusty sigh as they both openly ogled the display.

"Hold on, what? Moose?" Georgia asked, confused. She could've swore Tenny had been looking at *Levi's* ass when she said that, and…well, that just didn't make any sense.

"Oh yeah, Moose. Of course." Tennessee's cheeks were a little flushed, and she was staring at the far wall of the gym.

"Wha…wha…Please don't tell me you like Levi," Georgia finally stuttered out. Her mind could hardly grasp the idea.

Georgia had dated Levi for three years; she knew that he was a good-looking guy, and a nice one, too.

In comparison to Moose, though…

Choosing Levi over Moose was just plain insane, and that wasn't even taking into consideration the fact that Uncle Robert would have a heart attack if he knew.

"He's…" Tenny trailed off as her gaze shifted upward, apparently completely fascinated by the banner hanging from the gym's rafters that celebrated Sawyer's volleyball state championship in 1984. "Levi's just really different."

"And, in case you haven't noticed, *he's not Moose*," Georgia hissed. She was trying to point out the obvious without letting the panic overwhelm her, but she'd be the first to admit that she wasn't doing a very good job of it.

Tennessee *couldn't* like Levi. Tennessee was marrying Moose. It was the joining of the two reigning families in Long Valley – the owner of the local John Deere dealership, and the owner of the largest spread of farmland in three counties. Their children would be farming kings and queens.

It was settled. It had been their whole lives.

"Be honest with me for a minute," Tenny whispered, finally pulling her eyes away from the volleyball banner hanging from the eaves. "Have you ever seen Moose look at me like he wants to tear my clothes off?"

Georgia just stared at her normally meek and mild-mannered cousin with her mouth hanging wide open.

"Think about it," Tenny continued when Georgia didn't say anything. *Couldn't* say anything. "We've been practically engaged since we were born. Moose didn't have any more say in this than I have. Do you know what it's like to be forced into marriage by your *parents*?! It's like we're in the 15th century or something. Just because our dads are golfing buddies and BFFs for life doesn't mean that I want to marry Moose! And really? Moose? It's hard to feel attracted to someone named *Moose*."

"His name isn't Moose, it's Deere," Georgia protested

automatically, even as her mind was spinning, her gaze unfocused as she tried to take it all in. Tennessee didn't love Moose? Tennessee didn't want to marry Moose?

How was this even possible? Georgia was just sure that next, her cousin was going to announce that she was actually an alien from Mars. It would sound practically normal compared to what she'd just said.

"*I know what his name is!*" Tennessee whisper-shouted.

Georgia's head whipped back and her eyes finally focused on her cousin's face – beautiful and perfect and way prettier than Georgia could ever be. Tennessee probably could've made it in the modeling world if she'd wanted to. She had the kind of beauty that would stop a man in his tracks – *had* stopped many men in their tracks. Georgia had seen it happen again and again over the years.

She used to mind – being the Plain Jane cousin was not exactly something people tended to be thrilled about, and Georgia was certainly no exception in that regard – but she'd long ago moved past it. She would never be stunningly gorgeous like Tenny...but she also didn't have to spend two hours every day curling her hair and eyelashes, and wrangling every other hair on her body into submission that could potentially be plucked, curled, shaved, or straightened. She didn't have Uncle Robert as an overbearing father or Aunt Roberta as an overbearing mother.

She figured that all in all, she'd lucked out.

But tonight, she tried to look past the perfectly made-up face and hair and clothes, and into Tennessee's soul. It wasn't a view that Tenny allowed very often; she was agreeable and pretty and reasonably talented in music and cooking, and really, that was all that was required of her to become an excellent wife and mother to Moose's children. She didn't tend to present much else to the world, and it was a little weird for Georgia to *try* to see anything else.

"I hate the piano!" Tennessee burst out, a wild look in her

beautiful aquamarine eyes. "Hate it! You know who loves music? Virginia! She has more musical talent in her little pinky than I do in my whole body, and she actually likes her damn cello! If I never saw another piano in my whole life, it'd be too soon."

Georgia's mouth opened and closed a few times, trying to suck in air and not really succeeding. Hated piano? Who was this woman and what had she done with her cousin? Tenny probably spent two hours a day on the piano. How could she do that if she hated it?

"Laaaddddiiiieeeesssss and gentlemeeennnnn!" The voice of Kurtis Workman, the local microphone jockey, boomed out over the speakers, and the gym instantly grew quieter. If it was a gathering, auction, game, or any other event where someone needed to work a microphone, Kurtis was the person to call. He actually enjoyed every moment that he had a microphone in his hand, as weird as that seemed to pretty much every other person in Long Valley. And, let's face it, the world. "Tonight, we have the Sawyer Fire Department vs the Staff of the Sawyer High School facing off in this year's round of donkey basketbaaaaall! Up first, we've got—"

Georgia clamped down on Tennessee's arm and started dragging her towards the exit. They could laugh at overweight high school teachers trying to stay on the backs of stubborn donkeys some other time. Right now, Georgia and Tenny had some talking to do.

CHAPTER 6
GEORGIA

G EORGIA SUCKED on the water hose of her CamelBak for a moment, taking in the view below her as she tried to catch her breath. The sun was shining, the wind was registering at slightly less than hurricane strength, and there were a few balls of white dotting the deep blue sky. All in all, it was as pretty as a postcard. She looked across the wide valley to the Goldfork Mountains – the craggy, snow-covered tips reaching for the brilliant sky – and bit her lower lip. They were taller than the hills she was climbing, and thus still had a few wide drifts of snow on them. Maybe it'd be enough to get them through the year…?

The farmers didn't seem to think so, though, and neither did the state ag department. The official word put out by several farming organizations and the State of Idaho was that this was going to be a damn awful year to be a farmer (couched in more technical terms, of course). The credit union president had handed down the edict already – no large operating loans this growing season, period. Nobody was sure there'd be enough water to even get the crops to maturity, and farmers without crops…well, they were what you would call broke-ass farmers.

Not exactly prime lending targets.

Her breath was finally even again, and so she took off up the steep incline, keeping a close eye on the meandering trail as she contemplated the growing season stretching out in front of her. She was about to become persona non grata in the eyes of the local farmers, who would bitch and moan about how the credit union only wanted to loan to them when they didn't really need the help. Bankers and farmers were never going to be the best of friends, but this year was bound to be much worse.

Her foot slipped on a cluster of loose rocks and she scrambled for safer ground, swearing at herself as she went. She'd better pay closer attention to where she put each foot. The trail consisted of packed dirt with roots and stones sticking up everywhere, which meant one misstep could result in a broken ankle or twisted knee. She was so far into the hills at this point, there wasn't even a prayer of a cell phone signal; she'd lost that over an hour ago. If she got hurt…

She shoved the pessimistic thought away as she followed the curve of the trail, climbing ever upward. As she went, she automatically started to go through her to-do list in her mind, but then mentally came to a screeching stop when she came up empty-handed. She didn't have a to-do list, at least not today.

Honestly, it was a struggle to remember that it was actually a Wednesday, and not the weekend. The HR manager at the main branch had called over last week and had given her a stern talking to that she had too many vacation days piled up. She needed to take some time off, ASAP. In deference to the woman's "request," Georgia had put in for a vacation day today.

It still felt strange, though, and although she was enjoying her hike, a small part of her was glad that she'd only put in for one day. She could get back to work tomorrow. Top of the list was the report on vehicle loan defaults – if she didn't get that turned in soon, the main branch would be on her ass about that, also.

She didn't think that telling the head of the finance department that she'd been mandated to go on vacation by the head of the HR department would win her many brownie points.

She sighed. Someday, bureaucracy would be the death of her, she was just sure of it.

She spotted a movement out of the corner of her eye and she froze, her head whipping up. She was in bear country, and although she had bear spray on her, it was inside of her CamelBak. Not exactly convenient if a bear was about to charge.

But thank God, it wasn't a bear – only a dog. A Dalmatian, actually, with a beautiful white coat and faded black spots all over. He had fluffy ears, not smooth ones like the other Dalmatians she'd seen, but damn, he was gorgeous anyway. He was skittering along the tree line, looking over his shoulder at her as he slunk from bush to bush.

"Hi, handsome," she called out softly, holding out her hand and snapping her fingers. "What's a good-lookin' boy like you doing all the way up here? Where's your owner?"

The dog disappeared behind a thick tree trunk and then stuck his nose out the other side, staring mournfully back at her.

"You're a shy thing, aren't you," she said just above a whisper, trying to get closer to the dog without doing something stupid like stepping on a branch and sending him running off into the trees. "It's okay, I won't hurt you, I promise." She made some kissy noises, feeling a little ridiculous as she did it, but she figured most animals liked that sound. At least, she assumed they did.

This dog seemed to be the exception, though. He had moved again and was now trying to hide behind a larger boulder, apparently going with the "If I can't see you, you can't see me" line of reasoning. Unfortunately for the dog, his hindquarters were sticking out for all to see.

Not exactly stealthy.

As she got closer, she could see that they were hindquarters that seemed to be shaking, with the tail tucked up tight between his legs. Her heart broke a little at the sight. What had happened to the poor thing?

She stopped and rummaged around in her bag to find her stash of beef jerky. It was supposed to be her afternoon snack on the way back down the hill, but nothing spoke to a dog's heart like jerky, right? It had to work better than the kissy noises, anyway.

"Come here, boy," she whispered as she crept closer, holding the jerky out. "Come here – you'll like it, I promise!"

She could see his nose sticking out, wiggling in the strong breeze as he tried to weigh the promise of beef jerky against agreeing to get that close to Georgia to eat it.

"Who did this to you?" she whispered, moving ever so slowly towards the cowering dog. "And where is your owner? You have to have one – Dalmatians are too damn expensive to just be abandoned on the side of the road." She didn't know much about dogs, but even she knew that purebreds were costly. Not to mention that the dog had a collar on, although unfortunately there were no tags dangling from it. But a collar meant human ownership. So where was that human owner?

Just as she was almost to the boulder, she smelled it. Something…weird.

Well, not weird per se, not if it'd been June, anyway. But she was smelling the distinct odor of a campfire, which…out here in the wilderness at the beginning of May?

Just…*why*?

It was still way too cold to camp at night out here, and most roads were closed until Memorial Day. She hadn't expected to run into another soul on a weekday – not this far up, and certainly not at this time of the day.

But…her nose was quivering as much as the dog's. That *totally* smelled like a campfire. Was someone out here roasting marshmallows?

She straightened up and left the dog behind for a moment to work her way further up the trail to another outlook over the valley. *First I find a random-ass Dalmatian wandering around, scared to death of people, and now I'm smelling campfire smoke. This day is just getting weirder by the—*

And that's when she saw it.

A thick column of black smoke was rising into the sky from the pine forest below. Faintly, she could hear the pop and crackle of pine sap being boiled off by the heat, and through the trees, she spotted the occasional orange flame, dancing in the wind.

There was a wildfire raging through the forest.

Directly downhill from her.

More specifically, in between her and her car.

"Oh *shit!*" she gasped, unable to yell, her heart slamming against her ribcage as she tried to take it all in. A wildfire? At the beginning of May? Who'd ever heard of such a thing? Fire season shouldn't be starting until this summer, at the absolute earliest. There were no wildfires in May. It was against the law...or...or *something*!

"Oh *shit!*" she got out again, this time as a strangled cry. That damn dog...she couldn't leave him behind.

A Dalmatian out wandering in the wilderness and a wildfire roaring up through the forest.

Of *course*.

Her body wanted to go into flight mode and she felt the muscles tense up in her, readying to take off at a full sprint, but she fought the impulse. She could freak out later. She could panic and run in circles all she wanted, once she got home. Right here, right now, she couldn't afford to. She had to think through the problem logically. It was a puzzle, a puzzle that had to be solved so she could live.

So, a puzzle with life-and-death consequences. No pressure or anything.

She rolled her eyes at herself – sarcastic, even in the face of death – and forced herself to go through her choices. There wasn't a way to get down the hill, through that fire, and back to her car. Not gonna happen. She mentally tossed that choice out the window.

Staying where she was seemed like a pretty shitastic choice too, mostly because it appeared that choice would end in a fiery death. Not exactly the way she'd wanted to end her time here on earth. She mentally tossed that choice out the window.

Which really just left up the hill. She wasn't going to be able to outrun a forest fire, though, especially because the undergrowth was thick and she'd have to stick to the path. The fire wouldn't be forced to follow a switchback path up the hillside, though. *Damn cheater…*

And anyway, further up the trail were just more pine trees and underbrush and rocks – there wasn't exactly a fire-free zone she could go hide in—

Hold on – rocks! Eagle's Nest, of course!

It was a huge rocky cliff at the top of the hill with no vegetation around it. Ergo, nothing to burn. Ergo, the flames would pass on by.

Right?

That totally seemed like a valid plan to her, not in the least because she had literally no other choice.

She ran back up to the curve of the trail, and to the Dalmatian that was still cowering behind a boulder. Right where she'd left him.

"Come here, boy, we gotta go," she whispered urgently as she held out the now slightly slick piece of jerky, moist from the sweat on the palms of her hands, the smell of smoke growing stronger. Or maybe it just seemed like it was growing stronger. For all she knew, it had turned back the other direction.

Or, it was still heading straight towards her.

It was a 50/50 chance at this point, and honestly, she wasn't too enthralled with those odds. They were great odds when it came to winning a lottery; not such great odds when it came to surviving.

The dog crept forward slowly, his nose going a million miles an hour as he smelled the jerky. *Come on, come on, come on…* Finally, he snatched the jerky from her hand and began to dash for the boulder.

"We gotta go!" Georgia hissed as she grabbed the dog's collar, stopping him in his tracks. He whined, panicking, as she began pulling him up the trail behind her, the dog fighting her every step of the way.

Yeah, this was fun.

She worked her way up the trail, the smoke and smell from the fire growing stronger by the moment, and she realized her 50/50 shot at the flames going a different direction was rapidly dwindling before her eyes. Her heart was beating a million miles a minute, and she couldn't seem to catch a full breath, but dammit all, she was almost there and she'd be safe – maybe – if she just hung on a little longer…

She burst out of the trees and shrubs, her heart pounding as she stared up at Eagle's Nest. Years before, a pair of golden eagles had nested in the cliffs here, and the name stuck. There weren't any eagles around anymore, but that was no reason to change the name.

She headed for the dead center of the rock face, figuring that this would get her the farthest away from any brush or anything burnable at all. The dog's feet scrabbled on the rock underneath them as she pulled him along but she ignored his whimpers of protest. "It's for your own good," she informed him as she forced him forward.

That's when she heard…a plane? A helicopter?

What the hell?!

She stopped for a moment, her hand firmly gripping the dog's collar, as she squinted up into the sky. Sure enough, there was a helicopter flying overhead.

That was it, she'd officially seen it all. Even as her mind was trying to figure out why a helicopter was flying around, she was waving her free arm in the air, trying to catch its attention. They could swoop in and pick her up.

Okay, so maybe she'd watched too many movies, and that wasn't actually possible, but dammit all, they had to help her *somehow*!

The blades of the helicopter only whipped the flames up higher, though, and then it peeled off and headed back out, its path lost in the haze of the smoke. Georgia's shoulders slumped. She was by herself again. Well, her and a dog that was scared spitless of her.

So yeah, by herself.

She dragged the dog over to the rock face where she laid down, squishing herself up against its cool expanse, and pulled the dog up next to her, her arm slung over it, holding it tight against her.

Water!

Like an overturned turtle, she fought to get her backpack off, but finally, she pulled it up over her head, yanked on the zipper, and grabbed the bottle of water that she'd brought along as backup to the CamelBak water. She ripped the top off and began dousing herself and the dog liberally with it. Anything to keep sparks from catching fire on their hair or her clothing.

Sparks…Sparky…

"It'll be okay," she told Sparky as he shivered and spasmed next to her. She wasn't sure if it was from fear of the fire or fear of being next to her, but it hurt her heart either way. "We're gonna be all right," she told him firmly. "No need to panic."

She didn't have time to pull the backpack apart and get the water pouch out so she could douse them with it also, so she just pulled it back over her head, trying to shield her face from the heat and flames that were roaring up the mountainside. It sounded like a train, barreling down the tracks towards her, and just like in a nightmare, she was trapped against this rock face, unable to escape, unable to move.

The next time the credit union insisted on her taking a vacation day, she was going to spend it in bed with a book. At least then she had a fairly good chance of living through the "vacation."

That was, if she lived through this one.

CHAPTER 7
MOOSE

OOSE WIPED his hands on a grease rag as he stood back from the 4440 in front of him. A quick re-priming of the fuel system and it should be good to go back out to the Nash place—

Three long beeps blared out of the radio clipped to his belt, causing Moose to jump a little in surprise. *Dammit!* The emergency responder radio got him every time. It would end up taking ten years off his life, he was just sure of it.

"Attention all Sawyer City firefighters," intoned Mr. Behrend, the city's very old and very grumpy dispatcher. "There is a wildfire out northwest of town, up in the hills. The county fire department has asked for assistance in fighting this fire. I repeat, all Sawyer City firefighters…"

Moose tuned out his emergency radio for a moment as he looked around the work bay, frantically trying to find the shop manager, Sam. He spotted him in the corner, sifting through their parts pile. "Sam, fire! I gotta go!" he hollered, even as he began sprinting for the door. His boss called something back, but it was lost beneath the radio chatter breaking out.

"Base, this is Levi Scranton. I am in the Horseshoe Bend

area, but I am on my way back now. I'm at least an hour out. Over."

A crackle and then, "Base, this is Chief Anderson. I am heading to the station now. Over."

Moose slid into his truck, jamming his keys into the ignition. He'd wait for the chatter to die down and then call himself in. He'd beat Levi to the station, but not by much. The dealership was on the opposite side of the valley from Horseshoe Bend, and was also quite a bit out of town. By the time he got to the fire station and suited up, he'd be on the second fire truck to leave, for sure.

"Who spotted the fire? Over," someone asked. It sounded like Dylan, Luke Nash's employee. He hadn't been with the volunteer fire department for very long, and even over the radio, Moose could hear the excitement in his voice. Moose laughed a little to himself, the adrenaline pumping. There was always a thrill that came with being called out, that was for sure – a thrill even he couldn't deny. Fighting fires would never grow old.

The radio crackled and then, "Wildlife biologists were in a helicopter, doing a count of deer and elk, when they spotted the smoke column. Hold." The radio fell silent. Moose was on a tear towards town, cursing how far out the dealership was from the fire department, the city, and life in general, when the radio came to life again. "They are reporting that there is a person and a dog on scene, up at Eagle's Nest. I repeat, there is someone up at Eagle's Nest, and it appears that there is a dog with them."

Oh shit, shit, shit!

Moose took a hard left up a country road, his tires squealing on the pavement as he headed out towards Eagle's Nest. Sure enough, as he leaned forward and peered through the windshield, he could detect a faint column of smoke rising up in the sky ahead of him, from the foothills.

Forget his gear. He didn't have time for that shit. Moose was closer to Eagle's Nest than anyone else because it happened to be on the dealership side of the valley. By time he drove all the way into town and over to the firehouse, threw on his suit, and rode back out with the rest of the crew, this guy and his dog would be long dead.

Moose couldn't follow protocol, knowing that he had the chance to save someone if he didn't.

Dammit, why was some dude out hiking in the foothills today? It was nice enough weather for spring, sure, but didn't he have a job to be at or something? It was too early for it to be a tourist – they almost never showed up until after Memorial Day.

Whatever. He needed to call Jaxson before he lost all signal. Leaving the chattering radio beside him on the passenger seat, he pulled his cell phone out of his pocket. Jaxson answered, sounding out of breath. "You on your way?" he asked, not even bothering with a greeting.

Moose didn't either. This was no time for pleasantries.

"I'm on my way to the fire," he said bluntly. "I'm not coming to the station beforehand."

"What?!" Jaxson roared. "You can't go fight a fire single-handedly! And without equipment!"

"I know," Moose broke in, before Jaxson could get a full head of steam on him, "but I'm not going to. I know Eagle's Nest – I can get up to it from the backside. No fire truck is going to be able to reach this area, which means we're going to be fighting this with Pulaskis and chainsaws. By the time you guys get the fire under control, this tourist is gonna be dead. I'll go up the backside of the foothills and over the top, down to Eagle's Nest, and get the guy and his dog out."

Jaxson started to protest again, but this time, Moose just bluntly cut him off. "Jaxson, I'm gonna pull local boy card here. I know this place like the back of my hand. I'm already a lot closer to it than y'all are, because I was at the dealership when the call came in. I can make a difference. You gotta trust me."

And then the phone was beeping in his hand and Moose

pulled it away from his ear to see "No Signal" flashing on the screen. "Dammit!" he growled, putting the phone into airplane mode before dropping the worthless hunk of electronics into an empty cup holder. He didn't know how much of that Jaxson had caught.

His radio had gone silent also, which Moose did *not* take as a good sign, but he snagged it from the passenger seat and tried to radio in anyway.

"Moose Garrett to base," he said.

Nothing.

He let out a curse that'd set his grandmother's hair on fire if she'd heard him, and tossed the worthless radio into the backseat. After 9/11, the federal government had made a concerted effort to get radios into the hands of all first responders that should work anytime, any place, anywhere, and most fire departments had taken advantage of that grant money to get a top-notch radio system for their crew.

Every fire department, that was, except for the Sawyer Fire Department.

He cursed former Chief Horvath as he slammed his hand down on the steering wheel. The man had been in that position for far too long, and had just gotten damn lazy. Anything that smacked of paperwork, he'd done his best to duck. He'd bought that overpriced, brand-spanking-new fire truck a couple years back, and ever since then, he hadn't even bothered pretending that he was interested in doing more. He'd done his part, he'd stayed the course, and from there forward, he was just biding his time until he could retire. Filling out pages of paperwork to get the new radio system sounded like way too much work for a lazy guy like Chief Horvath.

Well, with any luck at all, Jaxson would've heard most of what Moose had said, and wouldn't panic too much. He needed to focus on getting the rest of the guys out to fight the fire. Moose could take care of himself.

The road shrunk down to one lane, and then pavement

disappeared completely and Moose was bouncing along on a rutted dirt road an elk would be horrified to walk down. He grunted in pain when he was bounced up high enough that his seatbelt locked, slamming him back down into the seat.

The good news was, his truck was as tough as shoe leather, and a 4x4 to boot, so it'd climb a greased pole if need be. He could get pretty far up the backside of the hill that dropped off into Eagle's Nest before he'd be forced to get out and climb. Any mile he could drive, he would. It would shave precious minutes off his arrival time, and right now, every minute counted.

Finally, he reached the row of boulders that he couldn't wind his way past. This was where the truck ride ended and the hiking began. He shifted into park, and jumped out to begin his search through the backseat for supplies. The first thing he reached for was his emergency backpack. Part of his first responder training had been to always carry a backpack with water, snacks, and extras like matches and a couple of space blankets, just in case he was ever trapped out in the wilderness unexpectedly. He wasn't going to attest to the freshness of the food, but hey, beggars couldn't be choosers.

He unzipped the front pocket and pulled out the headlamp he kept tucked in there, pulling it into place on his head. He didn't need to turn it on yet, but having it ready to go could only be a good thing. The sun was starting to head for the western horizon, which meant that they were about to enter the seemingly endless twilight zone that came along with living in a deep valley. For hours after direct sunlight would've disappeared, the sky would still be lit with the fading rays of the sun.

Hopefully Moose would be able to get the guy and his dog back up to the truck and to safety before the light completely disappeared, but that was nothing more than a hope at this point.

Actually, he realized as he squinted towards the column of

black smoke rising into the air, twilight was going to hit a lot earlier than usual today. This fire was big enough that the haze from the smoke was going to block out most of the sun they could otherwise normally count on.

He cursed as he slung his backpack over his shoulder and then began searching for the rope he'd thrown in the backseat last fall. Stumbling around in the dark with a tourist and dog in tow was not his idea of fun.

"Rope, rope, rope," he muttered to himself, pawing through the junk. He'd kept meaning to get it out and put it away, but somehow, he'd never gotten around to it. His laziness was about to pay off. He tossed some blankets and an old jacket out of the way when he finally spotted it, peeking out from under the seat, and pulled it out, sighing to himself as he did.

Dammit, it was as short as he remembered, which meant that it was too short to get all the way down to the base of Eagle's Nest. He'd gone out rock climbing and rappelling with Levi dozens of times over the years, and this spot was a favorite of theirs, so he knew just how much rope he needed to get to the base. This wasn't going to do it.

But on the other hand, if he didn't rappel off the side of the cliff, he'd be stuck taking the trail on the north side that also wound its way through the forest to the base of the cliff. It was totally doable, of course, but a hell of a lot slower. He might as well have just come with the rest of the guys in that case.

No, down the front was the only way. He could get the dog, the guy, and they could hike back out together the long way around.

His heart was running at top speed, adrenaline dumping into his system on overload, as he climbed up the barrier of large boulders, his work boots slipping as he tried to heave himself upward. This climb was a hell of a lot easier when he was wearing the right shoes. No surprise there, of course.

He finally got to the top of the boulders and worked his way over to a relatively skinny boulder stuck firmly in the ground. It was the same one they'd tied off to countless times in high school. The boulder wouldn't move an inch, so he at least had that certainty he could count on, even if it was the only one.

He didn't have rappelling gear or safety equipment of any kind, and he was risking life and limb, but hell, he'd come this far. He could go a little farther, right?

He straightened up and took a moment to look out over the hillside and valley below. Smoke and flames were billowing up, but it appeared the majority of the fire had started working its way to the south. *Thank God.* It wasn't terribly surprising – daytime winds tended to go upslope and then as soon as evening hit, they usually changed directions and went downslope. It looked like that was holding true for the winds whipping this fire up. As long as this tourist and his dog had stayed put at the base of Eagle's Nest, they might just live through this after all.

As Moose was doing his best to figure out where this fire was going and what it was doing, his boot slipped a little on the pebbles underfoot and he instinctively looked straight down, his eyes skittering past his boots and down the cliff face. He'd made it a point to never look down – he hated admitting to it, but heights scared the bejesus out of him, something even Levi didn't know. Looking over the valley was one thing; looking straight down a cliff was another.

And that's when he spotted her.

"Georgia?" he said, in shock.

CHAPTER 8

GEORGIA

THERE SHE WAS, huddled against the cool of the rock, trying not to breathe in too deeply, holding Sparky close against her, praying harder than she'd ever prayed in her life that the fire would change directions and leave her the hell alone, when she heard a loud noise over the roar of the wildfire.

Rocks, bouncing down the side of Eagle's Nest.

What the hell? What knocked the rocks loose?

She wiggled backwards a little until she could give herself enough room to crane her neck upwards – not her most graceful move ever, but okay – to see a dark figure waaayyyyy up at the top of the cliff face.

He looked down and their eyes locked. Her mouth dropped open as she stared upwards.

"Georgia?" he called down to her. "What the hell are you doing here?"

"What am *I*—" She broke off into a coughing fit, the smoke starting to burn her lungs. She'd been careful to keep her shirt over her mouth and her head tucked down between the rock and Sparky for what felt like forever, but now that she'd pulled away from that sheltering embrace, the ash and soot were starting to work their way into her lungs.

She tore her eyes away from the apparition of Moose – she was at least 72.3% sure that he was a figment of her smoke-addled mind – and towards the fire below. She hadn't dared to lift her head before, and she was shocked to see that the fire had in fact turned and was heading south. There were glowing embers everywhere, and a few straggly brushes still on fire, but God must've been listening, because she was still alive.

She sat up fully and leaned against the rock face, holding onto Sparky firmly with one hand while she rummaged for her CamelBak hose with the other. Flipping the cap off with one hand, she brought it to her mouth and sucked down the divine liquid.

"Ahhhh…" she sighed, leaning her head against the rock and closing her eyes. She sucked on the hose again, happy to be swallowing something that wasn't red hot and glowing and trying to burn her alive.

Sparky trembled as he sat next to her, whining every few minutes, *clearly* upset about being this close to Georgia. She pushed the lid back into place on the hose and then began stroking Sparky slowly and softly.

She told him he was okay, it was all right, he'd live through it, she'd take care of him…just a soft murmur of comforting words to soothe the poor thing, and honestly, to soothe herself. Now that the fire had moved away, she could feel the belated panic and fear begin to worm its way inside of her. She could've died. By all rights, she should have. The red glowing embers in front of her suddenly seemed like the glowing eyes of wolves, and she felt the panic tightening her throat, shortening her breath, she should've died, she should've—

A rock bounced down the cliffside and landed with a clatter next to her, scaring the hell outta her. She jerked and stared upwards to find Moose rappelling down the side of the cliff using the rattiest piece of shit rope she'd ever seen in her life.

Wha…

Her mind blanked.

Oh Lordy – he was *real*. Her mind had completely dismissed him as some sort of weird illusion, and through the sticky veil of panic and fear that she was desperately trying to push down, she realized that she'd somehow banished him from her mind once she'd decided he wasn't real.

It had to be shock. Nothing else made sense. It was all hazy and blurry and she began shaking as hard as Sparky, huddled up against the cold rock, getting colder yet as the sun began to set behind the Goldfork Mountains, and nothing was making sense and she was stroking Sparky harder and faster, telling him again and again that he would be okay because he would be okay, and maybe she would be okay too, and—

Moose's arms were around her and he was pulling her up against his broad chest as she began to weep violently into his shirt. Her mind was spinning even as she cried, going in endless circles, and she wanted to tell him what had happened and ask him how he got there, but she couldn't. As fast and as relentless as her mind was, her tongue would not move at all. She was trapped in a world of silence as she sobbed her guts out, relief and panic and joy and terror flowing through her, endlessly through her.

Finally, the river of tears and sobs slowed down, and she began trying to work her way out of the world of panic she'd wrapped herself up in, and back to the land of the living. And Moose.

"What am *I* doing here," she finally croaked out, as if a tsunami of tears hadn't hit between the last words they'd spoken to each other, "what are *you* doing here?"

He let out a deep laugh as he pulled her closer to his side. "You're something, you know that?" he said softly as he held her to his side.

"That doesn't answer my question," she informed him through her snuffles. "Was it the helicopter?!" she burst out when the memory floated to the top, through the layers of panic still swirling through her. "I thought they'd abandoned me for dead."

"Yeah, it was them. A bunch of wildlife biologists doing a deer and elk count to see how the herds did during the winter. They were flying low when they spotted the fire, and when they swooped in for a closer look, they saw you."

"I guess I should stop cursing them and their grandchildren then," she said with a small laugh through her tears, and Moose let out another deep laugh.

"I'd put the voodoo doll away if I were you," he said dryly. "So what's up with the dog? I didn't know you had one."

Georgia pulled away from the warmth of his body to look around. Hold on, where had Sparky gone? During the flood of tears, she'd somehow lost her grip on his collar. She spotted him at the edge of the rocky area, pacing back and forth as he looked out at the still-smoldering ground and bushes.

"Not mine," she said with a shrug. "I found him as I was hiking the trail. I was in the middle of trying to get him to come to me when I smelled the fire. He's skittish as all hell; I think he's been abused. Who leaves a Dalmatian out in the middle of the wilderness? Whoever his owner is, I don't think he ought to get him back."

"Are you sure it's a Dalmatian?" Moose asked, squinting through the rapidly darkening twilight.

"I don't know. It's white with black spots. Doesn't that make it a Dalmatian? I don't know much about animals; my mom was allergic to dogs."

"Hell if I know," Moose said, pushing himself to his feet. "My mom was allergic to the messes that dogs made."

She let out a little snort of laughter at that as she watched Moose try to get close to the dog. It whined and moved out of range, clearly not happy about having Moose so close to him.

At least he doesn't hate just me…

Right then, she heard the low thump-thump-thump of

helicopter blades cutting through the air, and she shot to her feet, craning her neck to see past the pine trees stretching up into the sky. Was the helicopter back to rescue them? It came into view, flying low, its blades whipping up the flames again further down the hillside. Moose hurried to the center of the rocky clearing and held his hand up in the air, jutting his thumb up clearly. The helicopter tilted towards him in acknowledgement and then headed back out, the comforting thump-thump-thump of the blades disappearing along with it.

Georgia longingly watched them go. Didn't they have a rope ladder they could throw out the window or something?

Moose caught the disgruntled look on her face and let out a small chuckle. "The fire officials were probably going crazy over the idea of a civilian out here, and me without any sort of equipment. That was just a recon mission to make sure we were okay. Dropping a rope ladder out of the side of a helicopter is only something that happens in movies."

Her mouth opened and closed a few times – how did he know she'd just been dreaming about a rope-ladder rescue?! – but she finally nodded grudgingly. "You're right. Hanging onto a rope ladder while swinging through the air, suspended from a low-flying helicopter…I'm not sure my nerves could've handled that anyway."

"Even military personnel with special training get freaked out over that sort of thing," Moose pointed out. "They're not going to subject a civilian to it."

"True," she grumbled. She didn't have to be happy about it…

"Well, I'm going to look at the fire in the area for a minute. Stay put," he tossed over his shoulder, and then leaving Sparky and herself behind, he headed down the slope. He wasn't gone long before he came back, hurrying through the blackened brush. "Damn hot!" he said, dropping to his knees and unlacing his boots as soon as he got to the ring of rock. He kicked them off, brushing at his feet ruefully. "Well, that was stupid, Moose," he mumbled to himself.

"So I take it we're not going back down the hill to get out of here?" Georgia called out.

"Not unless you brought fireproof footgear with you," he called back, scooping his boots up and starting to limp towards her in just his socks. "It got hot enough to begin to melt the rubber of the soles on my boots, so I'm pretty sure your tennis shoes aren't going to fare any better."

She stared ruefully down at her Nikes. "Probably not," she said with a disgruntled sigh.

He settled down next to her and wiggled his toes. His socks – which had probably started out white this morning – were gray and black with soot, small holes burned in them from the heat.

"I think I owe you another pair of socks," she said with a small laugh. "And boots, too."

He shrugged, the fading light making it hard to see his face clearly. "No biggie. We should talk about our plans for tonight. I'm assuming your cell phone doesn't work?"

She shook her head. "I lost signal a couple of hours ago."

"Yeah, I lost it on the way up here too. Even the first responder radio doesn't work."

"Aren't those supposed to work anywhere?"

"The new ones do," he said, his jaw tightening with anger. "But we don't have the new ones. Chief Horvath didn't do the paperwork for 'em. Jaxson is hard at work, trying to get us caught up, technology-wise, but there's so much to do…I used to like Horvath, ya know? Thought he was a pretty good guy. I knew he wasn't getting everything done like he was supposed to, but it wasn't until he was gone that I found out how much he'd left 'for later.' He wanted to just play with fire trucks – ride them in the 4th of July parade and throw candy out to the kids. Work? Not his strong suit."

Georgia nodded. That sounded like Chief Horvath all right.

He was a portly older gentleman that she'd seen around town, but had never had much reason to talk to a whole lot. But she'd heard from more than one source that the closer he got to retirement, the less he cared.

Right now, she wished he'd cared a whole lot. A working radio would be a godsend.

"So, our choices are to hike out, around Eagle's Nest to the north. We can't climb back up the cliff 'cause there's no way to reach the rope."

She craned her head to look up the rock face in the gathering darkness. A rope dangled, high above their heads. Moose'd made quite a drop to get from the end of that rope to the ground. She'd seen it when it had happened, but had already forgotten. Her mind still felt fuzzy around the edges, and there was a part of her that knew she was still in shock.

"Or," he continued, "we can stay put for the night and hike out come morning. I think that's what we ought to do, considering the path outta here isn't exactly paved and smooth. We could break our necks hiking it in the dark, and it'll be pitch dark by the time we get to the truck."

"It honestly doesn't sound like we have much of a choice," she said ruefully, and then shivered, her whole body spasming from the force of it.

"Dammit, Georgia, you're freezing to death," Moose cursed, grabbing his pack and riffling around in it. "I think I still have the space blankets in here, and probably a sweatshirt." He switched on his headlamp and began pulling items out, most of it unrecognizable to her in the quickly fading light. Finally, he pulled out a beat-up plaid button-up shirt.

"Here, put this on over your t-shirt," he said, holding the garment out to her, his headlamp turning with him and blinding her. She instinctively held up a hand to block out the beam of light and he let out another curse. "Sorry," he said, switching the headlamp off before holding up the shirt again. "It's not winter gear, but it's better than nothing."

She gratefully slid her arms into the sleeves and was instantly swallowed up by the sheer size of it. She knew Moose was physically bigger than her, but she hadn't realized just how much bigger until now. She could detect the faint smell of his cologne, just peeking through the campfire and smoke smells that were overpowering them.

It smelled…nice. Comforting in a part of her soul that she hadn't paid attention to in a very long time.

She pushed that thought away. That had to be the smoke and shock talking.

"Let me see what else I have," he said, flipping his headlamp back on and digging in again. He came up with two pathetic-looking peanut M&M packages, a small package of beef jerky, and a bottle of water.

"Well, we at least won't die of dehydration," Georgia said, taking the proffered package of M&Ms and tearing into it. Moose switched his headlamp off and settled in next to her to feast on his own M&M dinner. She shifted on the ground, her ass going to sleep from sitting on the hard rock. "I have water in my CamelBak also. I had a water bottle too, but I threw that water on top of Sparky and me."

"Sparky, huh? Cute name for a girl."

"What?" she said, shocked. "Sparky isn't a girl. He's a guy."

"Only if she's had a sex change and is now sporting different equipment than she was born with," Moose said dryly.

Instinctively, Georgia's eyes searched for the dog in the darkness, but even as she strained to see him…her, she knew it was useless. It was just too damn dark in the wilderness, with no street lamps or cars passing with their headlights on, or business signs lit up. She'd forgotten how dark it got at night out in the middle of nowhere. It made her feel helpless and small. Not exactly a feeling she relished.

She shifted on the hard rock again.

"I guess I didn't look, now that I think about it," Georgia admitted. "I just assumed it was a boy."

"Why, because boys don't know how to stay put where they're supposed to?" Moose asked with a laugh as he finished his package of M&Ms and began searching through his pack again.

"Probably." Her voice was light as she said it, but her body betrayed her and she shivered again. She didn't know if she was cold from sitting on a rock that was endlessly sucking her body heat away, or if it was because it was night, or if it was because she was still in shock, but she couldn't seem to stop shivering.

And then Moose was shaking out a large, crinkling piece of something and laying it over them, pulling her tight up against his side, sharing the warmth of his body with her. His hand was caressing her head, pulling it down to his shoulder, running his fingers through her hair. He was saying something in a low voice but her mind refused to register what it was.

She could've died. By all rights, she should have. Hiking by herself up in the hills with no cell phone signal? What a stupid thing to do.

Stupid, stupid, stupid.

Even as she berated herself, she felt herself sinking into the heat of Moose's body. He was so warm and protective, like a grizzly bear, there to guard over her. Nothing bad could happen with him there.

Once she'd stopped shivering so hard her teeth were in imminent danger of chattering right out of her skull, she could actually hear him. "Shhhh...it's okay..." he murmured, and her mind flipped back to when she'd been holding Sparky close to her, trying to calm ~~him~~ her down even as the wildfire raged towards them. She'd been so strong in that moment. What'd happened to that strength?

And then she remembered the promise that she'd made herself – she could fall apart as soon as she was safe. She'd imagined that this safety would be in her bedroom at home, but for tonight, it was in Moose's arms instead.

Moose, who was forbidden to her.

Moose, who was practically engaged to her cousin.

Moose, the one man she couldn't marry.

She shouldn't be snuggled up to him out here in the darkness. True, Tenny didn't actually want to marry him but since she'd apparently never told Moose that, let alone anyone else, they were still as good as engaged. Georgia couldn't let herself fall in love with Moose any more than she already had.

But still, she stayed in the circle of his arms, leaning against him, smelling the wildfire and pine trees and him. Completely reliant on him, when she was normally so very independent.

At that moment, she couldn't seem to make herself regret it.

Later she would, but not right now.

CHAPTER 9

MOOSE

MOOSE WOKE UP SLOWLY, a particularly persistent bird call bringing him up through the layers. He was disoriented – why was he sitting outside? And why couldn't he feel his arm?

He looked down at his left arm, which was when he spotted Georgia snuggled there beside him, her mouth slightly open as she snored softly into the pre-dawn darkness.

Georgia. The fire. It was all coming back to him now.

Except the feeling in his left arm. That wasn't showing up at all. If he didn't move his arm and soon, he wouldn't have a left arm *to* move. He tried to pull back just a little at a time, hoping to keep from waking Georgia up.

Even as he tried to extricate himself from her snoring embrace, he was also mentally pinching himself. Waking up next to Georgia was the most wonderfully awful thing he'd ever had happen to him in his whole life. Having her there, nestled against him, relying on him, believing in him…

He shouldn't let himself go there, of course. Mentally, he couldn't afford to. Georgia was so far off-limits for him, she really ought to have *No Trespassing* tattooed across her forehead.

He was going to marry her cousin. Someday. When he could make himself do it.

But right here, right now, it was just them against the wilderness. There was no cousin, no guilt, no responsibilities weighing him down. He could just be him – the him who wanted nothing more than to lean down and kiss Georgia on her soft lips.

Well, maybe he wanted to get his arm out from underneath her a little more than that. It was starting to hurt something fierce.

He tugged a little more, Georgia snuggled closer a little more, gave a little sigh, and then, her eyes drifted open and she was looking up at him. The world froze in the flat, pre-dawn light as they stared at each other, their mouths just inches apart, and he wasn't breathing but he was leaning down—

"Woof!" Sparky said softly, her legs pawing at the air, in the midst of one hell of a dream. Georgia and Moose jerked apart and they were laughing, acting like it was no big deal as Moose rubbed his arm, trying to get some circulation back into it, and they scooted apart, turning to look down over the valley, pretending that nothing had happened.

Nothing at all.

"What…" Georgia yawned and stretched, making his piece-of-shit holey flannel shirt look better than it had any right to, "what time is it?"

"I'm not sure," he admitted. "I left my phone in the truck 'cause it had no signal, and I don't wear a watch."

"Shit," she said, pulling her bag across the rocks over to her, "I forgot to put mine into airplane mode once I got out of range. I bet it's dead as a doornail after spending all last night searching for a signal." She pulled the phone out of the front pocket of the bag and heaved a sigh. "Yup. Nothing. Not that it would do us much good, but it'd be nice to at least know what time it was."

She began shaking from the cold, and with a muttered curse,

Moose tucked the space blanket in around her again, the material crinkling with each movement. He had no clue who thought that space blankets were a good idea, but after last night's ordeal, he was going to find a small fleece blanket to pack in his bag instead. He felt awful that this lightweight piece of crinkling shit was the best he could offer Georgia.

Some rescuer he was.

"Sorry," she said around chattering teeth, "I was fine, but you know how it is when you get out of bed in the morning. The shock of the cold air…"

Even as her body was jerking violently from the shivering, she was trying to straighten out her hair, running her fingers through the silky blonde strands, and Moose had to bite down – hard – to keep from telling her to stop.

She made the just-waking-up look…well, look damn good. He wondered for a moment what Tennessee would look like first thing in the morning, when she hadn't dolled herself up and curled her hair and primped for hours in front of the mirror, and realized that not only could he not imagine it, he didn't *want* to imagine it. Beauty-pageant looks were attractive to a lot of men, but Moose was beginning to realize he absolutely wasn't one of them.

He preferred gutsy, athletic, muscular, short blondes who didn't mind going after what they wanted, and worked damn hard to get to where they were. You could even say that he had a type…that is, if being in love with Georgia Rowland was a type.

"What?" she asked, breaking into his thoughts, and he jerked his eyes up to hers. "What's wrong?"

"Wrong?" he echoed numbly, while his mind spun in circles. *Love? I'm not in love with Georgia.*

"Yeah, you're staring at me all funny." She said it with a smile on her face, but even through the battle waging within him, he could tell she was confused.

I'm marrying Tennessee and I don't want to. There, I said it.

Buuuuttttt, there are a lot of things in life that I do even though I don't want to. It's called being an adult. I can't duck my respons—

"You there?" Georgia was waving her hands in front of his face and he was jerked back to the present. Again. He was starting to feel slightly seasick, honestly.

"Ummm…yeah. Sorry. Didn't sleep well last night." Which was a total lie. He slept better than he had in ages, snuggled down next to Georgia, her soft curves pressed against him.

There was something he was not going to admit out loud. Ever.

"Well, do you think we should try going back downhill through the burned-out area, or on the side path up to the top?" Georgia was obviously focused on getting out of there, and even though his dick was urging him to go back to the part where they'd almost kissed, he had to admire her single-mindedness. *Someone* needed to be thinking with their brain, not with parts south of the border, and that someone obviously wasn't gonna be Moose.

He pushed himself to his feet to get a better look down the hill. He let out a heavy sigh at the blackened wilderness in front of him. "Honestly, I don't want to walk through that. Even if it looks like the fire is out, we could kick up embers as we go, and start it up all over again. I think we need to take the side path up to the top of Eagle's Nest to where my truck is, and then I can drive you back to your car. I'm assuming it's at the bottom at the trailhead?"

"Yeah. Man, it seems like years ago when I parked it and started hiking. I can't believe that was just yesterday morning." She stood up and wrapped the crinkling space blanket around herself, moving to his side to look down the hill too. She had this little stripe of dirt on the tip of her turned-up nose, and he shoved his hands into his pockets to keep from reaching out to her and wiping it off.

Off limits.

Georgia Rowland is off limits.

He only had to repeat that to himself another 7431 times before his brain would finally believe it.

"Well, let's get to it," he said, focusing on the topic at hand. "I'd like to call Jaxson and tell him I'm okay. I'm worried that they're going to waste time and resources trying to save us, so the sooner we get moving, the better."

The light was growing a little brighter as the eastern edge of the valley began to lighten. He could see her face easily now – the smudge of ash across her cheek and nose, the soot on her arms and legs. Despite his best intentions, he reached out and instinctively wiped the ash on her cheek away, and then his hand jerked like he'd touched a hot ember.

He busied himself brushing the pebbles and dirt off his jeans until he got himself under control. If just touching Georgia on the cheek was getting him into trouble…

He was up shit creek.

They both turned and looked at Sparky at the same time, who was a fair distance away, curled up on the rock, watching them carefully.

"How did you get Sparky up here with you?" Moose asked as he began to pack his stuff away into his bag and lace up his boots. The sooner they got off this hill and back to civilization, the better. Back to his almost fiancée, who he was totally going to propose to soon. That's who he needed to focus on.

"I dragged her," Georgia admitted with a small laugh. "Maybe a dog would know to run away from a forest fire, I don't know. But I couldn't take the chance. I would've felt awful if she'd been burned up in all of that. She wasn't exactly happy about it, though, and I'll admit that there were a few times that I was tempted to give up and just make a run for it. Whoever did this to her ought to be taken out back and shot."

Finished gathering everything up, including the empty wrappers from their M&M's feast, Moose slung his backpack over his shoulder and said, "Well, hopefully she'll be willing to follow us out of here this morning. I don't particularly want to drag a 50-pound dog through this trail we're about to go on."

Georgia sucked on her water hose for a moment, and then smiled up at him. "I'm ready to go. Let's see what happens."

They headed down the path to the north, stopping and checking occasionally to see if Sparky was following along behind them. She was, although she was careful to keep her distance. It was going to be interesting to see if they'd be able to get her into the truck once they got back there.

Well, one problem at a time. No reason to borrow trouble, right?

"So you never told me why you were up here hiking yesterday," he tossed over his shoulder as they huffed their way up the switchback trail. "Doesn't the credit union need you at work?"

"You would think, wouldn't you," she said, and even though she was trailing behind him and thus he couldn't see her, he could practically hear the disgruntlement radiating off her in waves. "I was basically forced on this little mini-vacation by the head of the HR department at the main branch. Apparently, it's against company policy to let people accrue too many vacation days because if I quit suddenly, they'd have to pay out all of those days to me. So I was ordered to take some time off. Honestly, next time I am forced to take a day off, I think I'm going to spend it curled up in bed, reading a book. The chances are pretty damn good my house won't catch fire while I'm laying in bed. Well, at least, I hope not!"

He chuckled at that, even as his mind focused on the idea of watching Georgia, curled up in bed, wearing an old t-shirt without a bra on and short shorts (hey, it was his daydream – she could be wearing whatever he wanted) and he could sidetrack her from her book by offering to keep her busy doing *other* much more…entertaining things, and—

He shook his head at himself. He'd spent his whole life sorta kinda okay with the idea of marrying Tennessee, just like he'd spent his life thinking that PB&Js were fine to eat for lunch. Not exciting, not grand, but…okay.

For the past couple of weeks, though, he seemed to be struggling with keeping himself in that mindset. Why was he suddenly rebelling against an idea that he was taught along with his ABCs? When he'd hit puberty, he'd started to question it a little more, but he'd never let himself go down that road too far. Tennessee deserved to be happy, and to have a husband who wanted to be married to her. He didn't get to question whether or not he wanted this. It would just be.

"How's your dad going to take you missing so much work?" Georgia asked, huffing along behind him. The air was thin and cold this high up, and even someone as athletic and active as Georgia was struggling with the steep incline.

"Good question," Moose said sarcastically, his own breath short and choppy from the strain. It was a worry that had been gnawing at him ever since he woke up this morning. His father wouldn't be worried about Moose's physical safety and wondering why he didn't come home last night, but he would be pissed when Moose didn't show up at the shop at 7:45 this morning like he was supposed to. "When the call came in yesterday, I was at work. Dad knows that I'm on the fire department, of course, and although he isn't happy when I leave work to answer a call, we came to an understanding a while ago that this is one of the things that I get to do." *Hopefully he remembers that understanding…*

"That's not always an easy agreement to come to with your father," Georgia said softly.

Are my problems with Dad this obvious to everyone?

"No, not always easy," Moose agreed, trying to keep the pain out of his voice. Maybe everybody could guess at the problems between his dad and him, but he didn't need to actively broadcast them for the world and verify for them that their guesses were right.

"When Levi and I were dating, he told me that your dad was

paying for his schooling, so he could afford to become a TIG welder. With Levi's father…" Moose could almost hear the shrug Georgia gave. "It definitely wasn't going to happen without your dad's help. I always thought that was so nice of him to see the potential in Levi, instead of just dismissing him because of his…background."

Moose just nodded, not trusting himself to speak. If he did, the truth might come out and it was a dark, bitter, ugly truth that no one needed to hear.

If Georgia could think positively of his dad, well, that was a good thing. Someone ought to be able to.

They fell into an easy silence as they followed the meandering trail, each lost in their own thoughts, occasionally looking back to make sure that Sparky was following along behind them. She was, although no matter how many times Georgia made that kissy noise and snapped her fingers, Sparky refused to get within arm's reach of either one of them.

Getting her into the truck is gonna be a bitch.

Speaking of the truck, he spotted it in the distance, parked at the base of the giant boulders that he'd had to climb last night.

"Almost there!" he said, wiping the sweat off his brow. The sun was just starting to peek over the horizon but he was already sweating up a storm. He really needed to get out and exercise more often. He was hellaciously out of shape. Doing oil changes on combines did *not* count as exercise.

The trail widened as it flattened out, and Georgia was able to fall in step next to him. She had a light sheen of sweat on her forehead too, but she didn't seem quite as out of breath as him. Not surprising, if a little damaging to his ego. Georgia regularly ran marathons, something he could only dream about doing. His father would kill him if he took that much time off work.

"So how are we gonna get Sparky into the truck?" Georgia asked as they neared it.

"That's what I've been wondering. She doesn't hate human beings; she's just scared of them. So she *probably* won't bite if we make a grab for her. Did she try to bite you at all yesterday while you were dragging her up the trail?"

Georgia shook her head, her flushed cheeks and glowing skin giving her the appearance of a Greek goddess. Goddess of Exercise and Sex.

Pull it together, Moose.

"No. She whined a lot, and she pulled against her collar, but she was never aggressive. I got her to come to me using beef jerky, and then I snagged her collar. Do you have any jerky left?"

"Yeah, I was saving it just in case we were stuck out here for another day or something." He slung his backpack off and pulled the Ziploc baggie out of the front pocket. "Let's see if she'll come to me."

He shook a little piece out into his hand and held it out for Sparky, clucking his tongue and talking softly as she circled him, trying to find a way to get the jerky without actually coming up to him. She was probably starving, and a part of him felt bad for using that hunger against her.

Despite that, she wasn't willing to grab for the jerky. She was hungry, just not *that* hungry.

"Don't take this personally," Georgia said softly after a while, standing off to the side and watching his fruitless efforts, "but the chances are damn good that whoever abused this dog was a male. Statistically speaking, anyway."

Moose straightened up and looked at Georgia, feeling the impact of her words like a punch to the stomach. She was right, although he hated to admit it. It didn't say much about his gender – much that was positive, anyway – that was for damn sure.

"She might be more willing to come to me," Georgia continued, when Moose didn't say anything. "And, we did bond a little when we huddled together at Eagle's Nest to escape the fire."

He nodded and held the jerky out to her. Her reasoning was

spot-on, even if it made him feel a little dirty, a little sick at the idea that just because he was a male, a dog would automatically assume that he was also an animal abuser. Not pissed at the animal for making the assumption, but pissed at his fellow men for making it a reasonable belief to have.

He moved off to the side and watched Georgia get to work. She dropped to her knees in the dirt and sand, holding her hand out with the prize in it, waiting quietly for the skittish animal to come up to her. "It's okay, pretty girl," she cooed, as Sparky got closer and closer, her nose quivering in the early morning light. "We just need to take you back to town. We need to find someone to love you, all right?"

Sparky whined a little, and then her head darted forward as she tried to snatch the jerky from Georgia and run before she could be caught. Georgia's hand snagged her collar just in time, though, and despite the fact that Sparky was fast and strong, jerking Georgia forward to land face first in the dirt, she refused to let go. The poor dog strained to get away, paws scrambling in the dirt, her prize in her mouth, but Georgia had a death grip on the collar.

A part of Moose wanted to bellow with laughter but he instead ran to Georgia's side, scooping the large dog up into his arms and carrying her to the truck before Sparky could drag Georgia halfway to Georgia. He heard Georgia roll over in the dirt, sputtering and laughing. "Thanks a lot, Sparky," she said between the spits in the dirt. "Next time I decide to save a dog from being burned to death, I'm gonna keep this in mind."

Moose laughed even as he struggled to keep Sparky contained in his arms. She was strong and damn determined to get free. His laughter turned to a grunt of pain when Sparky hit a particularly…sensitive spot with a back paw. "Halp!" he croaked, his voice cracking like he was 14 all over again. If he didn't put Sparky down, and quick, his ability to engage in… certain activities in the future was going to be greatly curtailed.

"Oh, sorry!" Georgia yelped, and he heard her scramble to

her feet and hurry to his side, throwing the back door of the quad cab open. Moose shoved the dog inside and slammed the door shut, then bent over, hands on his knees, as he tried to quell the pain radiating through him. The world went a little black around the edges, but finally, he could at least straighten up.

Georgia was sending him a painful smile of sympathy, and he grimaced back. "It's…I'm…it's fine," he finally got out. "Thanks for your help."

The pain settled down to a dull roar and he looked at Georgia, checking her over for scrapes and bruises. She seemed fine, other than being covered head to toe in dirt and sand. He began brushing at it, trying to help her clean off but then his hands were going over her tits and he jerked back.

Well, everything was still in functioning order.

Down, boy, down. Now is not the time.

Not that it ever would be the time with Georgia.

He ignored the pang of pain that lanced through him at the thought. "Ready?" he asked her, and when she nodded, he headed around to the driver's side, slinging his backpack off and throwing it into the bed of the truck, Georgia following suit with hers. "We have to move fast; we can't let her out." Georgia nodded her understanding, and on the count of three, they both flung their doors open. Whining, Sparky hesitated, trying to decide which door to jump out of, but her hesitation cost her the opportunity, and they were both inside with the doors shut firmly behind them before she could go anywhere.

They burst out laughing, the kind of laughter that bubbles to the surface after a hugely stressful experience, as Sparky whined, pacing back and forth in the backseat.

"All in a Thursday morning," Moose said with a cocky grin as he started the truck.

"You sure know how to show a girl a good time," Georgia said dryly, flipping the passenger side visor down and using the tiny mirror embedded in it to get the majority of the dirt off her face.

"Hey, when I showed up, you were in eminent danger of being burned alive," Moose pointed out as they bounced their way down the rutted dirt road and towards civilization. He'd left that piece of shit rope tied to the boulder at the top of Eagle's Nest, but he wasn't about to chance letting Sparky escape into the world just to go back and get it. He could retrieve it some other time. "I figure anything after that has to be considered an improvement."

"That's true. Dining on the finest cuisine of crushed peanut M&Ms, being dragged through the dirt by a dog that's terrified of me, and almost freezing to death right after almost being burned to death. Best vacation I've ever been on!"

As they both laughed again, Moose had to hand it to her – Georgia had a grand talent of making light of even the worst situations.

It was a talent he admired. Honestly, she had a lot of those.

He was beginning to wish that she didn't, though. It would make his duty in life a hell of a lot easier.

CHAPTER 10
GEORGIA

ONCE THEY WERE within cell phone range, Moose called Jaxson to tell him that he was all right and he had Georgia with him, and then called Adam Whitaker, the local vet, to find out if he'd be willing to come to the fire station to look Sparky over. Adam agreed easily and Moose hung up.

"Dammit, Georgia, I just realized that I should drive you down to your car at the trailhead," he said, his forehead crinkled with worry, "but I don't want to risk letting Sparky escape while we're in the middle of nowhere. She's only gonna fall for the 'come here to eat this beef jerky' ploy so many times before we won't be able to lure her anywhere with the promise of food. Would you mind if we took Sparky to the fire station first? I'll drive you up here to pick up your car afterwards, I promise. I'd just like to get Sparky checked over; I'm worried her former owner might've done internal damage or something."

Georgia's heart squeezed at the care and attention that Moose was showing a dog he'd only just met; a dog that had done her best to castrate him just a half hour ago. Not every guy would be so focused and worried about a random dog's well-being.

Just one more thing to admire about Moose.

"Sure, no problem at all," she said lightly, and she meant it. And, bonus points: She'd be able to spend just a little more time with Moose. There was an unreal quality to last night and today – no responsibilities, no connections, just them against the world. She wasn't ready to let go of that feeling yet.

Or let go of Moose.

She thought back to her conversation with Tenny the night of the donkey basketball fundraiser. How on God's green earth did Tenny look at Moose and Levi, and then pick *Levi*?

That just seemed…bizarre. Wild. Strange.

Sure, Georgia had made that exact decision in high school when she'd started dating Levi, but on the other hand, she also wasn't actually given a choice.

Moose had been off limits to every girl in school except Tennessee. It had been that way his entire life. They went to prom together. They went to concerts together. Tenny went to the football games and cheered Moose on…literally, what with being the head cheerleader and all the last two years they were in high school.

Moose and Tenny had been two peas in a pod their whole lives.

No, Georgia hadn't been given the choice between Moose and Levi. She'd been given the choice between Levi and nobody at all – dating choices weren't exactly numerous in the tiny town of Sawyer – and so she'd chosen Levi.

He was a good guy, absolutely. He just wasn't Moose.

Until the day she died, she wouldn't understand how Tennessee's brain worked, and that was a fact.

Her mind started to drift and her head started to bob as they made their way back towards town, the sway of the truck lulling her to sleep. Leaning up against a rock cliff, snuggling up against Moose's side…it wasn't exactly an ideal sleeping arrangement, even if her pillow was Moose. The stress and exhaustion of it all rushed over her, wearing her out. She felt like she'd been wrung out and hung up to dry.

Endless time passed and then they were coming to a stop and Georgia was struggling to open her eyes. Blearily, the fire station came into focus in front of her. "We're here," Moose said quietly, as Sparky's whines kicked up another notch. A small part of Georgia's brain remembered that Sparky had stopped whining and had settled down during the ride back to town, probably realizing that it didn't do any good to try to get out while the truck was moving down the road.

But now that they were at their destination, Sparky had gone back to whining and worrying again.

Georgia pushed herself to turn in the seat, stretching for a moment even as she reached into the backseat to pet Sparky. "You're fine, you're just fine," she crooned to the pacing dog. Not surprisingly, Sparky didn't seem to believe her. She looked back at Moose. "What's our game plan?"

"I think you ought to crawl into the backseat and hold her. I'll get out and open the door and drag her inside with me. I should've thought to ask Adam to bring a leash with him. We can't just keep dragging her around by her collar. Even a dog that hasn't been abused doesn't appreciate that."

Georgia nodded, her heart twisting a little inside at his words. There was no other explanation for Sparky's behavior other than abuse, but it still hurt to imagine that someone would do that to such a sweet, pretty dog.

She climbed over the console and into the back, which caused Sparky to really kick up her whines of panic and distress, but she grabbed the dog, pinning it against the seat, a death grip on the collar while she cooed and petted her soft, silky hair with the other hand. "It's all right, pretty girl – it's okay. I promise. Don't you worry. We're gonna find someone who'll love you forever."

The front door of the truck opened and closed softly, even as

Georgia continued to talk to the panicking dog in a sing-song voice. "You're going to love Adam Whitaker, I promise. He's a real nice vet. He just needs to look you over—"

The door opened and Moose's hand shot out, snagging the collar in a death grip as Sparky scrambled to get away. Bent at the waist, he half walked, half dragged Sparky into the fire station as Georgia hurried after them. Once they got inside, she shut the man door behind them with a happy laugh – they'd made it.

Adam looked up from his conversation with Jaxson and came striding over. "There's the woman of the hour," he said softly to Sparky. He looked up at Moose. "Let's take her back into the supply closet. It's got that table in there for organizing, and it's nice and enclosed. She won't be able to run too far if we corner her in there."

Moose just grunted his acknowledgement, all of his concentration focused on getting the dog through the fire station without losing his grip on her collar. Finally, he got her into the closet and together with Adam, they got her onto the table. Moose looked back at the open doorway at Georgia and said, "She knows you better, plus I have to file some paperwork for last night's fun." He flashed a dazzling row of white teeth at her, and finished with, "You mind helping Adam out here?"

"No, not at all." She was happy to have something to do, actually. Just standing around and watching other people work wasn't exactly her style. Moose turned sideways and crab-walked out of the storage room as Georgia came the other direction, trying to stay out of his way but also not wanting to leave too much of an opening that would allow Sparky to make a dash for it. She was looking up and he was looking down and her tits were on fire and her breath had disappeared and then he was moving towards Jaxson to give him an update on what happened, and Georgia was doing her best not to melt into the floor.

If they had been alone, she was sure they would've kissed.

She *knew* they would've kissed. But they weren't alone and they should never be alone again. This just proved it.

She hastily shut the closet door behind her and hurried over to the examination table. It was beat to shit and looked like it'd survived a bombing raid or two, but it was at least sturdy, and for that, she was grateful. She petted Sparky, cooing and feeding her the small treats that Adam had slipped to her to keep Sparky entertained while he did an examination. As he worked, he asked Georgia what had happened – how she'd found Sparky – and she told him the whole story.

"Do you think Sparky would've run away from the fire if I hadn't been there to drag her away?" she asked Adam, worrying her lower lip as she did. "I kept questioning myself as I did it. She'd obviously been abused by someone and I didn't like forcing her to come with me, but I also didn't want to chance her getting burned to death."

Adam looked down at her – with his cowboy boots on, he towered over her – and gave her a kindly smile. "Whatever you did to get Sparky to come with you, I promise you that it was nicer than what her previous owner did to her. It's hard to know if she would've survived the fire or not, but even if she had, she wouldn't survive wandering up in the hills by herself for very long. One way or the other, she probably would've died up there without you. A little bit of being dragged around was worth her life, I promise."

She nodded. Adam was right, and that sure made her feel better about the whole thing. Forcing a dog into obedience rubbed her the wrong way, but it was a damn sight better than letting her die.

"All right, I'm done for now," Adam said, standing back from the table and the shaking dog on it. "I'm gonna open up the door and let her run around the fire station a little bit. If we give her some breathing room and let her explore on her own, she might start to realize that we aren't going to abuse her. We'll just have to make sure that when people go in and out of the fire station, they close the man door behind them quickly. Have you given her food or water yet?"

Georgia shook her head. "We didn't have any cups or bowls to pour water into, and I certainly didn't go hiking with dog food in my backpack." Adam gave a little chuckle at that. Georgia continued on, "I gave her a bit of beef jerky and so did Moose, but she's gotta be starving."

Adam nodded. "I'll tell everyone what I found. Michelle from over at the pound should be here soon. I called her as soon as I hung up with Moose. She can start the paperwork to do a rescue of Sparky."

He sidled past her in the cramped quarters, leaving her behind to continue to pet and soothe Sparky, but Georgia realized that the touch of his body against hers as he made his way to the door did absolutely nothing for her at all.

What a difference from the same exact situation with Moose just minutes before.

It sure didn't help Georgia's state of mind. The fact that she'd only reacted this way to one person in her entire life, and that person was the one person on earth she couldn't have…

Not exactly a happy thought.

Adam opened the door to the storeroom as Georgia let go of Sparky's collar. She went darting out like her ass was on fire, and Georgia just laughed a little to herself as she watched the dog streak from the room. Sparky was so sure she'd outsmarted them by escaping their grasp, but once she was out of the small room, she looked around the large bay, clearly not sure what to do with her newfound freedom.

Moose, who hadn't been let in on the plan yet, started sprinting for Sparky, who quickly dived under a fire truck.

"It's okay!" Georgia exclaimed before Moose could follow the dog under the truck. "Adam said to let her walk freely around the station for a bit. Just be careful when you open the man door so you don't let her outside."

Moose stopped in his tracks. "Oh. Right," he said, looking a little embarrassed, but honestly, Georgia was impressed all over again. She had no doubt that he would've crawled around underneath the truck, trying to chase the dog, just because he thought he was supposed to.

If there was one thing that Moose was always good for, it was doing what he was supposed to do.

"Do we have some sort of bowl here that we could give her some water?" Georgia asked, already heading for the small kitchenette, which basically consisted of a dorm fridge, microwave, industrial sink, and a few dusty coffee mugs.

"I'll get it," Troy rumbled, two steps ahead of her.

Georgia jerked to a stop. Troy spoke. Troy was there. When had he shown up at the fire station? She hadn't even seen him when they came in.

But Troy was already searching through the cupboards, looking for a bowl for the occasion, so Georgia let him have at it and headed back to the group of men, where Adam was discussing Sparky's condition.

"—viously mistreated by her previous owner," he was saying as Georgia came walking up. She found herself standing next to Moose in the circle of men. Not on purpose, of course. He was just there, and then she was standing next to him. Sometimes that sort of thing just happened.

"What I can't figure out," Adam continued, "is how did she end up in the hills like that, with no one around? Purebreds don't just show up in the wilderness, miles from the nearest human. Someone dropped her off or lost her or *something*. Georgia, were there any vehicles or anything out there before Sparky showed up?"

She shook her head confidently, and then stopped. "Honestly, I'm not sure," she said slowly, her brow wrinkling as she thought through it. "There could've been, actually. I was pretty high up in the hills, and off in my own little world. I was more focused on not tripping over tree roots and killing myself than paying attention to my surroundings. Sparky scared the hell outta me when I first saw her. I saw this movement out of the corner of my eye and I was just sure she was a bear." The guys all laughed and she grinned too. "Ridiculous, I know. It's amazing how quickly your mind flips through possibilities when you think you're gonna die. Anyway, it was soon after that the fire was roaring up the hillside, so I didn't exactly scout around for a vehicle."

Adam looked at Jaxson, and they both seemed to have the same thought at the same time. "A hunter," they said in unison.

"Some guy was taking a Dalmatian out to go hunting?" Georgia asked, totally perplexed. She wasn't exactly the world's biggest expert on dogs, but she'd never heard of a hunting Dalmatian. Weren't labs and retrievers usually hunting dogs?

"That's not a Dalmatian!" Adam said, laughing. "White with black spots...I can see why you'd think that," he said quickly, trying to spare her ego, but his eyes were definitely still sparkling with laughter. "Sparky's a setter. They're a really popular hunting breed. That's why her ears and her tail are so fluffy. Dalmatians are not fluffy – they're sleek and smooth all over."

"Not a Dalmatian, and not a boy. I really had this one pegged," Georgia grumbled to herself. Moose snorted with laughter.

Adam stared at her, confused. "What?" he asked.

"Nothing," she said, embarrassed she'd said that out loud. She waved her hand in the air dismissively. "So, our female setter here is a hunting dog. Why are you so sure that it was an actual hunter who lost her?"

"Well, it could be just a guy who happens to have a hunting breed, it's true," Jaxson allowed. "But the chances are pretty high that it was a hunter. It's been a dry spring, right? Just ask all the farmers. We shouldn't have forest fires this early, and it's only because there were a few patches of snow left around that the fire didn't totally rage out of control like they'd originally thought it would. That's why we're not up there digging trenches right now."

"So a hot tailpipe on a Jeep Wrangler or a pickup would set fire to the dead cheatgrass from last year," Adam finished. "It doesn't take much to start a wildfire in the middle of a drought, even if it is spring. The guy was probably off-roading, not paying much attention because he didn't expect to have anyone up there to see that he'd gotten off the trails, and Sparky ran away while she could. The tailpipe sets the cheatgrass on fire, the guy leaves before anyone can link him and the fire together, and the dog is left stranded up there by herself."

"Ohhhh…" Georgia said, tapping her finger against her teeth as she thought. "'Cause you get charged if you're found to have started a wildfire, right?" It all made sense. She'd thought a dog randomly appearing out of nowhere and a fire starting from nothing seemed strange, but she hadn't realized that they were two strange events that were linked. That made them a lot less strange and a lot more plausible.

"Yeah," Jaxson said dryly. "The government doesn't take kindly to having to pay tens of thousands of dollars to put out a fire that some jackass sets while out four-wheeling in places they're not supposed to go. But if this worthless sack of shit thought that it was okay to beat his dog, he probably thought it was okay to go hunting out where he wasn't supposed to be, and when he started a fire, he sure as hell wasn't calling it in. He split as soon as he could. He doesn't want to be on the hook for the damages that stem from a wildfire. That's probably why he left Sparky behind. He figured the dog would die or wander back home. I'm gonna guess he's a local boy, although I don't recognize Sparky. That doesn't say much for me, of course, since I only moved here five months ago. Does she look familiar to any of you?"

They all turned to search out Sparky in the corners of the station. Georgia figured she'd be hiding under a fire truck or behind a pile of equipment, but was shocked to see that she was instead sprawled out on Troy's lap, her tongue lolling out happily, a mostly empty bowl of water off to the side, as Troy quietly ran his hands over her fur rhythmically.

"What was it that you were saying about abused dogs not liking males?" Moose muttered under his breath to Georgia.

"No males except for Troy, I guess," Georgia whispered back.

Troy sensed the eyeballs on him, and he looked up from his pettings of the beautiful dog to see them all staring at him. "She likes me," he said simply.

Understatement of the century. Georgia would've been willing to bet money just a half hour ago that Sparky would take months, maybe years, to warm up to another human being. Seeing her with Troy was…eye-popping.

"Well now," Jaxson said with a small laugh, "I was gonna offer to keep her here at the station, but I think she ought to go home with you, Troy. Do you have a place to keep her?"

Troy nodded, his hands never stopping as they ran over the dog's completely relaxed body. "I'll figure somethin' out," he said.

Glory be. That was a whole four words in a row. Where did this talkative Troy come from? Was Sparky some sort of talisman?

Just then, the man door to the fire station opened, and Michelle Winthrop from the pound came bustling in. "I heard you almost got burned to death," she said, walking straight towards Georgia. "Are you okay?" She picked Georgia's hands up in hers, looking her in the eye as they talked.

"I'm fine, Michelle, I promise," Georgia reassured her friend.

"Good, good. Now, where's the dog?"

Georgia bit back her smile. Michelle liked humans; she loved animals. They came first, last, and always in her world. Asking Georgia how she was was a mere formality; something she had to do before she could get down to what really mattered.

A person couldn't take that the wrong way, of course, or

they'd hate Michelle. Animals were what mattered to her, and truly, Georgia was glad that the animals in the valley had such a strong and feisty advocate in their corner.

Michelle took one look at Sparky, still sprawled across Troy's lap, and stopped short. "I thought you said this dog was abused," she tossed over her shoulder as she took in the sight in front of her.

"She acted like it with me," Georgia said, moving to stand next to her friend. "She didn't want to come anywhere near me."

"What did you find when you examined her, Adam?" Michelle asked, slowly moving towards the pair on the cement floor.

"She has some bruises on her side. If I had to guess, just about the shape of a boot."

Michelle's face went dark, and Georgia could only be glad Michelle didn't know who the owner was. She really didn't want to lose her friend to a life in jail for homicide, even if the asshole deserved it.

"No broken bones, though," Adam continued. "The chances are pretty high that her lungs hurt from the smoke inhalation, but since I can't ask her, I don't know for sure. And for the record, she only stayed on the examination table for me because Georgia held her there. Her attachment to Troy is… unexpected."

"Especially since most animal abusers are male, statistically speaking," Michelle said baldly, bringing the dark and awful fact out into the open rather than shying away from it. Georgia was proud of her for saying it, rather than ignoring the reality that they all lived in.

Not, of course, that any man in that fire station right then was the kind of man who'd beat a dog.

Georgia looked up at Moose as he moved up beside her, concern in his eyes. He was afraid she was judging him with the broad brush of generalities, and her heart hurt a little at the idea. Moose wasn't capable of abusing a dog, end of story.

She reached out to squeeze his hand, and for a few glorious seconds, they were holding hands. A flush stole up her cheeks and she was staring at Moose, wishing with all her might that they were alone and she could finally kiss him—

"Are you gonna adopt her?" Michelle asked Troy, jerking Georgia back to the present, and to the fact that there was an audience in the room. Georgia pulled her hand away, embarrassed. If this got back to Tenny or Uncle Robert…

"Yes," he said simply, looking up at Michelle, not moving an inch lest he disturb Sparky.

"Good, good," Michelle said briskly. "Adam, were you able to tell if Sparky has been spayed?"

"No," he said, moving quietly to the other side of Michelle. They were standing in a half-circle around Troy and Sparky, giving the two of them plenty of room. Sparky was keeping a close eye on them, but was still content to lay in Troy's lap. At least for the moment. "I'd need to shave her to see if she has the scar, and I didn't think bringing a blade close to her belly right now was a stand-up idea."

"Good point," Michelle said, nodding firmly. "Well, Troy, I'm leaving her in your hands. When she's gotten a little more used to the idea that the world isn't out to get her, I want you to promise me that you'll take her on by to Adam's place to have her checked out. If she's not been spayed, you give me your word right now that you'll pay to have it done, or I won't let you take her."

Georgia bit back another grin. Typical Michelle right there. She said it how it was, and didn't shy away from the truth. She was kind, but blunt as a cement block.

"Promise," Troy said softly.

"Good, good. Well, I better get to it, then. Y'all just made my life easy. Troy, you take good care of her." And with that order, she marched off towards the door, ready to take on the world of wrangling the people and animals around her into submission.

"You'll need to get her a bowl and a leash and some dog food," Jaxson said. "You want to leave her here while you go to the store?"

Troy looked torn at the idea of abandoning Sparky, even if it was for her own good, but finally nodded. With a cluck of his tongue to Sparky, he got her off his lap and he stood up, looking down at his pants and shirt with a rueful grin. He was covered head to toe with Sparky's winter coat that she'd been busy shedding while he'd been petting her.

"Be back," he rumbled, and headed for the door. Sparky followed right on his heels until they got to the door. "Stay," he told her, and she sat down with a whine, watching as the door closed in front of her.

Suddenly, the last 24 hours hit Georgia like a ton of bricks. Her head swung a little drunkenly as she looked up at Moose. "Weshouldgogetmycar," she said, the words slurring together, her tongue refusing to cooperate.

He cocked an eyebrow at her.

"I think I ought to take you to Betty's Diner and get you fed," Moose said in a no-nonsense tone of voice. "You didn't eat lunch, dinner, or breakfast, and you're in no mood to cook right now. You'd probably nod off and burn down your house. While I'm driving you to Betty's, you're going to call Tripp and tell him that you're not coming in today. After I feed you, *then* I'll take you to your car."

Oh. Tripp. Her eyes flew to the clock on the wall. Holy shit! He was probably panicking right now. She was technically a no-call, no-show at this point. Not exactly professional.

Moose handed her his phone, remembering without her even needing to say it that hers was still dead, thumbing the button to unlock it so she could use it.

The home screen of his phone was a smiling pic of him and Levi together, holding up a stringer of fish. Tennessee was nowhere to be found. Georgia didn't know why she cared, because of course she absolutely positively shouldn't, but a small part of her was delighted to see that.

As she followed Moose obediently to the truck, too tired and hungry to protest about how dirty and smelly she was, and how she absolutely shouldn't go out into public like this, she called the credit union.

"Goldfork Credit Union, this is Tripp, how may I help you?"

"Tripp, it's Georgia."

"Oh thank God!" he hollered. She yanked the phone away from her ear instinctively but when he rattled on, she quickly pushed it against her cheek again. "—just kept going straight to voicemail and you've never been a no-call, no-show and I was damn sure you were dead and—"

"I'm alive, I promise," she broke in, realizing that if she waited for him to calm down to tell him what had happened, she could be waiting quite a while. "Did you hear about the fire east of town that broke out yesterday afternoon?"

"Oh yeah, a couple of customers were talking about that today."

"Well, I was up there hiking when the fire broke out. Just down the hill from me – between me and the car, actually. And there was a dog there, too."

"A dog started a fire?" Tripp asked, completely confused.

"No, her owner did. I'll tell you all about it later, I promise. I just wanted to let you know that I'm not coming in today. I hardly slept a wink last night, and I'm covered head to toe with ash and dirt, so I'm not exactly presentable. I'm going to take another vacation day. That should make HR happy." *Even if the loan department isn't.* That damn report wasn't going to write itself, which was really too bad. "Keep things running for me. I'll tell you everything tomorrow, I promise."

"Okay. Take care and sleep lots." He hung up and Georgia called the HR department next. Moose had driven them to the restaurant and they were now sitting in the parking lot, waiting for her to finish up before going inside. She sent him a smile of apology and he just shrugged.

The phone call went much faster with the HR department; she simply said that she was going to take a mental health day, and the head of HR sniffed her approval before hanging up.

"Don't you need to call your father?" Georgia asked, handing the phone back to him.

"I will in a minute. For now, let's get some food inside of you."

Georgia had to admit that this seemed like a stand-up idea.

CHAPTER II
MOOSE

THEY WENT WALKING into the restaurant and found his favorite waitress on staff, Chloe. Her platinum-blonde hair bobbed as she hurried over, tutting as she took in Georgia's appearance. Georgia was weaving a little on her feet from sheer exhaustion, and Moose had to stop himself from pulling her to his side to physically hold her upright. He absolutely shouldn't touch Georgia, but he absolutely, positively shouldn't touch her in *public*.

He couldn't hurt Tennessee like that. It wasn't fair to her.

"Oh darlin', just look at you!" Chloe exclaimed, reaching out and brushing at a streak of soot across Georgia's shirt. "I heard you got trapped up in the fire in the foothills, and don't you just look like it. I'll go get some coffee and creamer for you. Pick a table and I'll be right over." She hurried towards the coffee pot as Georgia drunkenly turned towards the booths, doing her best to act dignified. As if she had not quite literally been dragged through the dirt that morning and almost been burned to death the night before.

Moose gave in and took Georgia's elbow in his hand, supporting her as he guided them to a booth. It was just an elbow. No one would look at them funny for him touching her elbow.

Well, they would if they could feel the sparks shooting up his arm, like touching an electric fence that'd been turned on high. It was a damn good thing people couldn't read minds. Not even the gossip kings and queens of Sawyer could, for which he was eternally grateful.

Georgia sank into the booth across from him, her head drooping as she tried to prop her chin on a palm. Her blinks were growing looongeeer byyy theeee mooomeeent…

Her head snapped up and she blearily attempted to focus her eyes on his.

Moose had visions of her face-planting into a plate full of waffles. Normally, he'd just take her home to let her sleep this off, but he was half-afraid that part of her exhaustion was coming from low blood sugar because of not eating for so long.

She wasn't diabetic – at least that he knew of – but anyone who'd gone through the stressors that she had while also eating practically nothing for 24 hours could crash and burn. He had to get food into her, even if he had to spoon-feed her to do it.

Huh. On second thought, maybe he ought to get the food to go in that case. He could get away with taking Georgia by the elbow to guide her into a booth; he couldn't get away with spoon-feeding her like a toddler.

Chloe came up with the mugs and creamer and a pot of coffee. She poured a cup for each of them, sliding the creamer towards Georgia, and then said, "Y'all know what you want?"

Moose instinctively looked at Georgia – women always ordered first, of course – but her head was bobbing and jerking as she valiantly tried to stay awake…and not land face first in her coffee. If Moose was going to wait on her to make a decision, they'd be there a very long time.

"Two veggie omelettes with cheese and ham added," he said, not even bothering to open up the menus stacked at the end of the booth. "Biscuits for each; extra jam for me."

Chloe winked at him. "You got it. I'll tell Betty to move y'all to the front of the line. I'm afraid Georgia won't make it if we wait too long to feed her."

"I'd appreciate it."

They both turned to Georgia as she made incoherent noises, waving her hands in the air dismissively. He knew exactly what she was trying to say, even if her mouth didn't – she was fine. No worries at all. Just because she'd seemingly forgotten how the English language worked, she was fine.

Chloe took off for the kitchen while Moose just shook his head at Georgia, the laughter bubbling up inside of him. Her drive, her backbone, her willingness to put in hard work…it's how she became the youngest branch manager in Goldfork Credit Union history, and a female to boot. All of that was on display now, as she attempted to give off the illusion that she was in perfect working order.

He pushed her coffee cup towards her, encouraging her to drink it, and then realized with a frown that she hadn't put any creamer into it yet, and that just wasn't gonna work. She didn't touch black coffee with a ten-foot pole. As she put it, she liked a little coffee in her creamer.

He pulled the coffee mug back to him, added three little cups of french vanilla creamer, stirred, and *then* pushed it back across the table to her.

Georgia gave him a dazzling smile of gratitude, the wide swath of dirt across her forehead giving her a particularly pirate-y look, and promptly began downing the coffee. When she was close to the bottom, Moose waved Chloe over for a refill, then creamered it up for her again. She sipped at the second cup a little slower.

"Feeling any better?" he asked Georgia as Chloe brought by the biscuits with jam. He took over spreading the homemade jam and butter across Georgia's biscuit – even a butter knife in her hands probably wasn't a good idea at this point – and then pushed the readied biscuit over to her.

"Yeah," Georgia slurred unconvincingly, then hungrily dug into the biscuit. Moose eyed her cautiously. She in no way seemed better, although he supposed that she was at least speaking English now. Low bar, for sure, but she was clearing it.

He popped a bite of his own biscuit into his mouth and closed his eyes as he chewed ecstatically. He'd been so focused on making sure Georgia was okay, he'd been ignoring his own stomach growls, but now that food was arriving, his stomach was busy reminding him that he could eat a horse, with a side of cow, at this point.

It sure didn't hurt that Betty made the best biscuits in the area. The woman was a flat-out genius in the kitchen. There was a reason no one had tried to open a competing diner in Sawyer; Betty's fans were legion. If only she would stay open for dinner, Betty's Diner would be perfect.

She'd always maintained that she wanted her evenings off, though, so she wasn't gonna do it. Despite his selfish desire for her to be open past two each day, Moose had to respect that kind of surety and backbone about her business decisions competing with her private life. Wanting to strike a good balance between work and personal life wasn't something he'd seen modeled much in his own life.

"Here we go," Chloe said, sliding their oversized plates in front of them and then standing back with an appraising eye. "Ketchup? Extra butter?"

They both shook their heads, so with another top off to their coffee, Chloe was off to the races again. How she kept her energy level so high all the time was beyond Moose.

"So I kept meaning to ask," Georgia said after swallowing a particularly large and gooey bite of omelette, "how did the fundraiser go? Did you guys make some decent money? And who won the basketball game?"

"I can't believe you'd even ask that," Moose said mock-seriously, shaking his head in disappointment at her. He was secretly thrilled that she was talking, though. In complete sentences. With only a minimal amount of slurring. "The firefighters, of course. Although your dad put up quite the fight. He made two whole baskets during the game!"

Georgia laughed at that. "Wow! I would've put money on him not even playing," she said admiringly. "Go, Dad."

"How is it that you don't know how the game went?" Moose asked, digging into his omelette, veggies and cheese and ham oozing out. Hmmm…maybe he'd just marry Betty instead. Sure, she was pushing 70 and was as round as she was tall, but damn, could the woman cook. "You were there that night," he reminded her.

He'd met up with Tennessee at the fundraiser and they'd wandered around for a bit together until they'd spotted Levi and Georgia talking. His heart had…twisted or flipped or squeezed or something funny it probably wasn't supposed to be doing, when he saw them together.

Not that he'd ever admit that out loud, of course. He had no reason to feel that way.

None whatsoever.

"Uhh…Tenny and I started chatting, and then we wandered outside, and then ended up going home from there." Suddenly, she was studiously studying the table to her right.

A table that was empty, and not at all interesting.

Interesting…

"I'd wondered what happened. Tennessee just disappeared."

He was ashamed to admit that he hadn't even noticed until Jaxson had asked where she'd gone.

Also not something he was going to admit out loud.

When Georgia didn't say anything else, Moose prompted her. "What'd you two talk about?"

"Oh, this and that." She waved her hand in the air dismissively. "Cousinly sorts of things."

She was still staring at the table to her right.

"Hmmm…" he said noncommittally, suddenly wishing he

could've been a fly on the wall when they were discussing *cousinly* things, whatever the hell that meant.

But it was clear that Georgia wasn't going to fess up to anything else, so he moved back to the question she'd asked. "The spaghetti feed went really well overall, other than a couple of the older farmers complaining that we'd dare to feed them 'Italian food' instead of doing a baked potato buffet."

This caught her attention and whatever she'd been studying so intently at the empty table next to them was suddenly not interesting anymore. Her eyes jerked to his. "Are you being serious right now?" she breathed, and then started laughing. "Oh, Sawyer…there are days…"

"I know, right? I had to bite my tongue pretty hard over that one. But other than our daring choices of spaghetti and garlic bread, the event went well overall. A success for Jaxson out of the gate, and that's something that he needs. Despite what happened down at the bakery, what with saving Gage and Sugar from that fire and all, some of the older farmers still look at him a little askance. I don't know if they'll ever truly forgive him from moving in from the giant metropolis of Boise."

Georgia laughed pretty hard at that one, and then shrugged. "Tell him to join the party. I was born and raised here, but I'm also one of those dastardly females, so there are farmers who come in who refuse to talk to me about operating loans. Not only is Tripp good at his job, he's also a male, so I dump these guys off onto his lap when it happens. It used to piss me off, but now…" She rolled her eyes dramatically. "They're in their 70s and 80s, and still clinging to their farms. They're not going to change their minds about women in the workplace at this late date. They could overlook it if I was a secretary or something, but to be the branch manager…"

She shook her head in mock displeasure at the idea. Her smile was breezy and cheerful, but her eyes…they were dark and unhappy. She wasn't as good of an actress as she believed she was.

Moose wondered if anyone had ever told her that.

"I'm glad Tripp is good at his job," Moose said quietly, "but I'm sorry you have to use him as a liaison between you and the...older generation." Even as he said it, he thought back through the Garrett Tractor & Implement customers who came into the dealership every year. He could list off who he thought was giving Georgia a hard time, and probably be at least 90% accurate. They were plenty nice to him, being the owner's son and all, but these were the kinds of men who treated the shop guys poorly; who looked down at Levi as being inferior because of who his father was.

For being overall-wearing, tobacco-chewing, dirt-stained crusty old farmers, they sure could be judgmental as hell. It was one of the things he hated about the dealership.

Georgia shrugged again. "I realized a long time ago that if I'm gonna let that sort of thing get under my skin, I'd be crazy within the month. I just keep my head down and work hard and let them think whatever they want to think. The head of Goldfork Credit Union over in Franklin – he likes me and he knows that a lot of the complaints I get stem from my gender. I'm lucky to have a decent boss."

And with that, she let out a jaw-cracking yawn, looking across the booth at him with a bleary-eyed gaze. The food and coffee had given her a little bit of a pick-me-up, but there was nothing she needed now more than sleep.

"C'mon, let's go," Moose said, sliding out of the booth and waving Chloe down. He paid for breakfast, swallowing hard at the unexpected hit to his budget, and then guided a swaying Georgia out the front door.

Just by her elbow. Like a proper gentleman would.

"I feel like I hit a brick wall," she mumbled. "I was fine, and then..." She waved her hand in the air. "Now I's tired."

Moose let loose with a belly laugh at that. Georgia wasn't exactly an English schoolmarm, but her grasp of the English language tended to be pretty good overall. He was willing to bet next month's paycheck that she'd never said the word "I's" before.

He helped her into the passenger seat and then hurried over to the driver's side. He'd told her that he'd drive her out to her car after they ate breakfast, but looking at her doing the jelly-necked bob, he didn't trust her to drive at this point. All she'd need is to crash her car while trying to drive it home. That'd just make this week complete.

"What's your apartment number?" he asked, heading towards the Golden Ridge Condos. He knew she lived in there somewhere, but couldn't remember which condo exactly.

"Eleven," she mumbled, curling up against the passenger side door. He could only hope that she actually heard and understood the question and was telling him her condo number, and not how many times she'd read *Harry Potter* in high school. She always had her nose buried in one of those books, it seemed.

Or she could be telling him how many times she got into a fight with her parents in the 10th grade. Or how many times it took her to learn how to spell Mississippi. Or how many times she'd made love to Levi.

His smile instantly dropped from his face and he felt a little sick. Not at the idea of Georgia and Levi having sex – although undoubtedly the number was much higher than eleven, and no, that thought didn't exactly bring him joy – but because Levi was still in love with her.

Levi wouldn't cop to it, of course. He might not even be willing to admit it to himself. But if Levi knew how much his best friend craved being with Georgia…

Moose shoved the thought away with all his might. For the 98,281st time, he was marrying Tennessee. He had no choice in the matter. Georgia wasn't an option now, or later, or ever.

End of story.

He pulled up in front of her condo and then riffled through her backpack sitting in the bed of the truck, finally pulling her keys out triumphantly. He'd been taught to never go through a woman's things without her permission, but since Georgia was currently snoring up a storm, he figured he could be forgiven this one time. He zipped the backpack closed and slung it onto his back.

He opened up the passenger side door carefully, catching Georgia's limp body as she began to fall out, and slid her into his arms. She was short and petite, but that shouldn't fool a person; she was all muscle. She weighed more than she looked like she should, but after hefting tractor tires and parts around for years…hell, she was barely bigger than a mite.

He juggled the keys and her, finally getting the front door open and her inside. She snored a little and then nestled closer to him, completely oblivious to the world around her…

And completely oblivious to what she was doing to him.

He began hurrying through the house, pushing doors open with the toe of his boot as he went, wanting to put her down before he made a complete jackass out of himself. Despite the fact that she was dirtier than a hobo on a three-week bender, despite the fact that she was out for the count, it was still Georgia.

And holding her in his arms was the purest form of torture he'd ever lived through.

Finally, after discovering her office, her library, and a guest bedroom, he found her room – large and cheerful, a four-poster bed dominating the space with a small overstuffed chair in the corner by the window. A stack of books sat on the diminutive end table next to the chair, and more were piled on both nightstands on either side of the king-sized bed. His eyes skittered over the spines, unconsciously searching for *Harry Potter* titles, and then he stopped himself. He'd already broken into Georgia's apartment after riffling through her backpack without permission. He was not going to go pawing through her books next out of curiosity.

He gently laid her down on top of what appeared to be a

handmade quilt and then studied her soot- and ash-covered body. He could take her clothes off – it had to be more comfortable than sleeping in those dirt-encrusted things – but his gut told him that Georgia would rather sleep restlessly than have him strip her naked.

Not to mention that he *really* wasn't sure if his self-control could take it.

So he settled on removing her beat-up tennis shoes and then pulling a lap blanket from the end of the bed and draping it over her.

Quietly backing out of the room, he dropped her keys and backpack next to the entryway stand and headed out the front door.

It was time to go home, take a shower, and then he was off to work. Unlike Georgia, he didn't get to take a day off, and anyway, he didn't need one. He'd slept better last night with her in his arms than he had—

He stopped himself right there. Their little break from the world, where the rules didn't matter and he could look at her with the longing that he felt...it was gone. Done. Behind him, disappearing in the rearview mirror. They'd rejoined society, and he needed to come to grips with that.

CHAPTER 12
GEORGIA

S HE CAME AWAKE SLOWLY, stretching luxuriously and then stopping with a jerk halfway through.

What smells like a skunk made love to dirty gym socks?

Her eyes popped open and she kept her gaze locked on the ceiling as she took a tentative sniff of her armpit.

Oh Lord above, I stink!

She rolled out of bed and headed straight for the shower, keeping her eyes averted from the bathroom mirror as she went. She did *not* want to see what disaster was lurking in it. After all, if she didn't look, then it wasn't real. If it wasn't real, then she didn't have to face the fact that she'd sat in a booth down at Betty's Diner, in public, looking like she'd wandered in off the street after surviving for years in the wilderness without running water or electricity.

No siree bob, she did not want to look in the mirror, thankyouverymuch.

She stripped off her dirt-encrusted clothes, making a mental note to toss them directly in the dumpster, and then stepped under the spray of the relentless hot water, letting it pound down on her until she felt a little more human, scrubbing away at the dirt, watching it swirl down the drain. It was strangely satisfying to watch the dirt disappear and she was smiling to herself when, like an out-of-control freight train, it hit her.

The panic and terror began washing over her, drowning her, smothering her. One moment, she was fine, and the next she was sinking to her knees at the base of the shower, sobbing as the realization pounded against the inside of her skull of just how close she'd come to dying in that damn fire. She let a cascade of tears wash down the drain along with the suds and the ash and the dirt.

She'd never, ever thought something like that could happen to her. With just the slightest change in the wind direction, Moose would've found a charred corpse instead of her and Sparky.

She was shaking uncontrollably at the thought.

I wanna call my mom…

It was amazing, in a way, how she could be 26 years old, but when it all boiled down to the basics, she still wanted her mother when things went sideways. There was something about a mom that just couldn't be found elsewhere. Not in Tripp, not in Tenny, certainly not in her aunt or uncle, not even in Moose.

Not that she'd call Moose. The little interlude, where she got to pretend for a minute that it was she and Moose against the world, and it was okay for her to like how his eyes wrinkled in the corners when he laughed, and how his shoulders rippled with muscles when he did the simplest of tasks, and…

All of that was done now. Even though she now knew that Tennessee didn't actually want to marry him, that didn't change a damn thing. Her cousin wasn't willing to stand up to her parents and tell them no, and Georgia couldn't exactly do it for her. This was between Tenny and Moose (well, and her aunt and uncle and Moose's parents) and they all got to decide what to do and how to do it. Georgia had no say in it, and never would.

The two sets of parents would *never* be okay with Georgia

marrying Moose. She was the daughter of the poor Rowland brother; the one who'd inherited nothing at all. It was okay for Georgia to date and even marry Levi. It was okay for Georgia to run the credit union. It was okay for Georgia to care about who she married, and make the choice for herself…

As long as that choice wasn't Moose. That wasn't okay in any universe, alternate or otherwise.

Finally, all wrung out and cleaned up, she turned off the now-lukewarm water and pushed herself up from the floor of the tub onto unsteady legs. Toweling herself off, she faced the fact that although her desire to call her mom hadn't diminished one bit, she couldn't do it. Her mother worked as a lunch lady and playground monitor during the school year to bring in a little extra cash, and at this time of the day, she'd still be at the school. Georgia wasn't about to show up at the elementary school to sob into her mother's hairnet.

And anyway, she was trapped at home. She didn't remember a bit of it, but considering she was at her house and she damn well hadn't been capable of driving herself there, the only logical conclusion was that Moose had driven her back to her condo after breakfast, instead of out to her car. Considering everything after Moose paying for breakfast was a big blank hole, she was damn thankful to him for making that choice. She'd been in no shape to drive.

As grateful as she was, though, this meant she had to convince someone to take her to retrieve her car. She enjoyed a good marathon as much as the next person, but she didn't exactly feel up to a 20-miler today.

She took a quick look at her clock on her bathroom wall. Three o'clock in the afternoon?! She hadn't realized it was so late, but still somehow not late enough. The bank wouldn't close for another two and a half hours. She could wait for Tripp to get off and have him take her, but she was antsy, the desire to just *do* something roiling around in her.

After she got dressed in yoga pants and a t-shirt, she looked around her spotless house, trying to find a project to occupy her time. She rinsed out the bowl and spoon in the sink from breakfast the day before, and put away the basket of clean clothes waiting in the laundry room. She pitched her filthy, stinking clothes into the main dumpster for the condo complex, happy to close the lid on them and walk away.

And…she was now officially out of things to do. She looked at the clock again. Thirty-seven minutes had passed.

She closed her eyes and groaned. Normally, she'd curl up with a book and while away the afternoon with Tessa Dare's latest, but the thought just held no appeal today. She felt electricity shooting through her, an unsettled desire to do, to be, to move, keeping her from settling down.

She ignored the obvious thought pushing at the edges of her mind – that this was a sexual energy humming through her from being around Moose for two days straight – and decided instead to go for a walk. In fact, she could walk on down to the fire station which was only on the other side of town, and see if anyone there could drive her out to pick up her car.

Nobody in particular, of course, just…*somebody*. Moose wouldn't be there, after all. He'd be at work, trying to make up for the fact that he was late that morning to a puritanical father who did not tolerate such things. She was going to ask for a ride from any firefighter who happened to be on hand. Nothing more.

Plus, she could check up on Sparky while she was at it. Maybe Troy needed help with her. Not that Troy would ask for help if his hair was on fire, but she could go check it out for herself just to make sure.

She curled her hair and put on some makeup before deciding to change out of her yoga pants and t-shirt. She shuffled through her closet, picking out one of her favorite blouses that did its best to emphasize her not-so-generous curves and a pair of tight jeans that showed off her best asset –

her ass. She studied herself in the mirror, deciding that she looked good enough.

Of course you look good enough. You're just going to go pick up your car. You don't need to get dolled up to drive a car.

She pushed the thought away. After wandering through town looking like a runaway who hadn't seen the inside of a shower in months, it was only right for her to look nicer now. She had an image to uphold as the credit union manager, after all.

Nothing more than that.

She slung her purse over her shoulder, grabbed her keys from the entryway table where Moose had thoughtfully left them, and headed out. She walked the two blocks up to Main Street and then took a left, heading towards Boise…that is, if she kept walking for another week. Which she obviously wasn't going to do.

As she passed the Muffin Man Bakery, her stride slowed a little as she took in the carnage. From what she'd heard around town, Gage was still working on collecting the insurance money on it so he could start to rebuild.

Insurance companies…they were quick to collect their money, and slow to pay it out. If they didn't get a move on it soon, he should probably hire a lawyer to push them along. It'd been a month today since the fire had started; that was more than enough time for an insurance company to cut a check.

Seeing the soot-blackened walls and front windows sent a shiver down her spine in the bright sunshiny day. Sugar and Gage almost died in this fire; Georgia almost died in the wildfire. What was up with Sawyerites and fires lately? She let out a light laugh to herself. It made for a more exciting world than Sawyer usually occupied, that was for damn sure.

And then the laughter was gone and she was back in it again. She felt panic well up inside of her as flashbacks from yesterday's horror washed over her. Pinned between Sparky and the cliff wall, trying not to breathe in too deep, listening to the crackle and pop of the fire as it raged up the hill, just sure it would take her out too…

She stepped on trembling legs into a narrow alleyway and leaned up against the cool brick of the building, closing her eyes and breathing deeply, pushing the panic down, shoving it into oblivion, not allowing it to wreck her composure.

She couldn't let the flashbacks affect her like this. She'd lived. She was fine. She had nothing to complain about. She could stop being a pansy-ass on the topic right-damn-now.

She pushed away from the brick wall and continued down the street, shoulders back, head held high as she walked.

She was fine. She was totally fine. It was about damn time she started acting like it.

CHAPTER 13
MOOSE

Moose was in the middle of pulling a sickle bar out of the underbelly of a combine when his cell phone vibrated against his hip, letting out two soft bell tones that indicated whoever was calling was on his contact list.

Shit. He was already in deep trouble with his father for being hours late to work that morning; as he'd pessimistically expected, his father hadn't considered saving Georgia's life as being a valid excuse for Moose's tardiness. Moose had been keeping a low profile ever since, trying to stay out of the line of fire and out of sight of his father; all he needed now was to be caught standing around, jawing on the phone while he was supposed to be working.

But on the other hand, it was someone he knew; not just a telemarketer or salesman…

He snatched the phone out of the holder and swiped to answer before it could go to voicemail.

"This is Moose," he said, ducking behind a combine as he did so. Maybe he'd luck out and could hide from his father's eagle eyes.

"Hey, it's Jaxson. I have a favor to ask of you – Georgia is down here, hoping to catch a ride out to her car. I'm the only one here, or I'd have someone else take her, and I can't do it because I need to go home and check on Sugar. She keeps telling me that she's okay, but I think she'd say that even if one of her limbs had been somehow chopped off, *Monty-Python-and-the-Holy-Grail* style. 'It's just a flesh wound,'" he said in an atrocious English accent, mimicking the famous fight scene from the cult classic.

Moose let out a snort of laughter at that. He knew Sugar real well – they'd graduated from Sawyer High School together – and he figured that Jaxson just about had her pegged.

He could also replace the name "Sugar" with the name "Georgia," and be just as correct.

Women...

"Anyway," Jaxson continued, "I know you were late to work this morning and all, but I figured your dad understood under the circumstances, so I'm hoping he'll be okay with you taking some time off this afternoon, too. It should be a quick trip."

There was a rustle and some whispering, as if Jaxson had covered up the mic on his phone to talk with Georgia, and then Moose could hear him whispering, "It's fine, don't worry about it." More rustling and then Jaxson was talking to Moose again. "You good to head over here?"

Moose wasn't sure whether to laugh or curse or cry or scream or...or thank God above because he had an excuse to go spend more time with Georgia. Of course, if he did, there was a very good chance that his father wouldn't be talking to him by the end of the day.

Somehow, in that moment, he just couldn't seem to make himself care.

"Sure, sure, I'll be right over," he said, and hung up before he could change his mind.

Just as his finger was hitting the red button to end the call, he heard Jaxson saying, "I told y—" and then he was gone.

Moose would've laughed if he wasn't so damn nervous. Georgia knew better than to ask him to leave work early, especially after coming to work late, but Jaxson…he probably thought that with Moose working for his father and all, he could skip in and out of work any ol' time he wanted to.

And Moose wasn't about to inform him otherwise. It was embarrassing enough to have a father who worked him like a slave. He wasn't about to go advertising that fact to others.

He paused for a minute, considering tracking his father down and telling him that he was headed out the door, but he just couldn't.

It wasn't okay to sneak out the door. It wasn't okay to leave a job half-done. Mr. Hoffmeister wanted his combine back, like, yesterday.

But it also wasn't okay to be worked into the ground for the past 16 years. He was a grown-ass adult who was forced to live at home – who could be making more money down at Betty's flipping burgers – and the only thing that had kept him there all this time was the dangling of the dealership in front of him. That prize was always held up as the ultimate in life; what he should spend every waking hour striving for. The last time they'd talked about it, his dad had told him just five more years, and he could take over.

But he'd said that before, and somehow, the timeline had moved on him.

Would it be moved again? How long could he survive before he broke into a million little pieces?

Screw it. He headed for the shop door, his hands sweaty as he practically ran outside.

Freedom. It had never tasted so good.

His heart racing, he drove through town as if nothing was wrong – as if he hadn't just escaped the dealership like a convicted criminal would make a run for it. It was perfectly normal for him to drive a friend out to pick up her car. It was perfectly normal for him to have spent the night underneath the stars, huddling together and keeping from freezing to death.

Okay, maybe not *normal*, but he knew they'd done nothing

he wouldn't have done within full view of 5000 of his closest friends. He had nothing to be ashamed of, or worried about. And right now, he was doing nothing more than driving a girl out to pick up her car. He wasn't asking her to marry him or something.

So why did it feel so illicit?

Georgia's head snapped up when he came walking into the fire station, and she smiled nervously at him. She jumped off the tailgate of the water truck and came hurrying over. "I'm really sorry," she called out as she headed his way. "I tried to tell Jaxson that your dad would kill you if you left work early after getting to work late, but he has some really naïve ideas about you and your dad's relationship and wouldn't listen to me."

She arrived – breathless – in front of him. Her hair was curled, she had makeup on, and no dirt anywhere. She looked gorgeous, of course, which did absolutely nothing for his self-control. He smiled down at her, his heart racing with happiness even as the worry gnawed at the edges. He pushed back at it, fighting it down. Worry be damned. He was with Georgia again, even if only for a minute.

"It'll be fine," he lied, pretty convincingly he thought. "I'm not even sure if Dad will notice."

Two lies in less than 20 seconds. Nice…

He pushed that thought away, too.

"I'm assuming Jaxson already left to go check on Sugar?" he asked as they headed for the door.

She nodded. "He said you'd lock up after us, and he'd come back later."

Moose pulled the door shut, locking the handle and the deadbolt with his key he'd been given as deputy fire chief, and then they were off, headed for his truck.

"How was your dad when you got to work?" Georgia asked as she slid into the passenger seat. He shut the door behind her and took his sweet time rounding the front of the truck to his side, trying to think of what to say.

"He was...Dad," he said dismissively as he opened the driver's side door and slid inside. "Just like your farming customers who are stuck in their ways, so is my dad. He won't change." He shrugged, as if the browbeating he'd taken that morning hadn't stung. Hadn't bothered him a bit. "He is Rocky Garrett. If you expect him to ever soften up, you're gonna be sorely disappointed. So I don't expect it."

Georgia nodded, her gaze far away as she mulled over his words. "Your dad reminds me of my uncle," she said softly as they turned to head out of town and towards the trailhead. "I guess it's not surprising that they're two peas in a pod."

"They're so much alike, they'd either hate each other's guts, or be best friends," Moose said dryly. "I'm not sure if I'm happy or sad that they ended up as go-to-coffee-together-and-wed-our-children-to-each-other buddies instead of mortal enemies."

He was trying to pass it off as a joke, truly he was, but her little hiss of breath told him that she'd read right through that.

"It's gotta be hard to have a force-of-nature father," she said, her voice still quiet as she gazed out the window. They'd begun winding their way up through the foothills, but something told Moose that she wasn't watching the scenery as it passed. "Especially with him holding the dealership hostage until you marry Tenny."

"He *what*?!" Moose yelled, slamming on the brakes, tires squealing as they jerked to a stop in the middle of the road. He didn't care. He would damn well stop wherever he damn well pleased.

He threw the truck into park and pinned his gaze on Georgia. She stared back, eyes wide. "You don't get the dealership until you marry Tennessee?" she repeated, but this time it was a question, not a statement.

"When did you hear that?" he demanded, adrenaline

pouring through his veins. *I'm gonna kill that son-of-a-bitch with my bare hands, I swear I will. I'll tie him to a—*

"It's always been that way?" Her voice ended in a squeak this time. "Moose, please tell me you knew that."

"Of course I didn't know that!" he roared, his voice echoing in the cab of the truck as the anger throbbed through him. "I was supposed to get the dealership in another five years. *Nothing* to do with Tennessee. Where did you hear this?"

"Sunday dinner. You know I eat with Tennessee's family every Sunday, right? We switch back and forth between her parents' and my parents' house. Just last week, this came up at dinner again.

"Moose, I cannot believe you didn't know. It's...it's been that way since the beginning. For...for years." She was sputtering now, staring at him, eyes huge and pitying.

Pity...he hated that. He didn't want pity. He wanted revenge. Rage was boiling through his veins. *Bastard, bastard, bastard.*

All he wanted in life was to punch his father in the face – oh, what he'd give to do just that in that very moment – but Georgia was there. Not his father.

Georgia, who needed to pick up her car.

Body tense with rage, he jerked the truck back into gear and began heading up the winding hill again.

"He'd told me it would be five years for a long time now," he growled, more to himself than to her. How had he ended up in such a shitastic place? How had he been so damn stupid? "Oh, the irony...I was thinking just this morning that I didn't know if I could trust Dad that it really would be mine in five years, because he'd moved the goal post a couple of times on me. But I thought he was moving the date back because he didn't want to give up the reins and power of owning it all, not that he was secretly requiring that I sell my soul to the company store before I could inherit."

He let out a long sigh, trying to bring the rage under control and failing desperately. It was too strong, too overwhelming. The betrayal was too damn deep.

He whispered, "He knew that telling me who I had to marry was a bridge too far, so he didn't dare say this to my face. I wonder what he would've done if I'd brought home someone else as a fiancée? Would he have told me the truth then? I've always known marrying Tennessee was *expected*; I didn't realize it was *required*."

"Do you want to marry her?" Georgia demanded, turning in her seat to face him. "Do you want to marry Tennessee?"

Moose sucked in a deep breath. He hadn't expected her to be so blunt in her questioning, but then again, this was Georgia. She told it how it was. That was one of the many reasons why he lo—

Respected her.

And he'd show her that respect by telling her the truth. No matter how scary that was to him in that moment. He'd never told *anyone* the truth about this.

But it was about damn time to start.

"No. I don't. For the longest time, I had myself convinced that I did. Or at least that I could. But these last couple of weeks..." He shook his head, driving at this point more by instinct and feel than by sight. Thankfully these weren't busy roads, or he probably would've wrecked his truck by now. Staying in his own lane seemed like an awfully difficult concept at the moment.

He drew in a deep breath. "I don't want to marry Tennessee Rowland. I don't. I was going to because it was my duty as the oldest son and she's pretty enough and smart enough and she'd make someone a real fine wife, but...she's not for me." He blew out a breath and then began laughing, letting the hysterical laughter that was bubbling up inside of him loose. "I can't believe I'm saying this out loud. Look at this – my hands are shaking." He held his right hand out towards her, the tremor obvious.

She chuckled lightly, but her eyes were serious as she said, "You need to talk to Tenny. Right away."

He nodded, feeling a ball of dread grow in his stomach. He didn't want to hurt Tennessee – he never wanted to do that – but breaking things off with her after all this time…he *was* going to break her heart. He just had to face that fact. And his mom's heart. And his father's—

No, his father didn't have one. It was impossible to break what did not exist.

"You're right," he said firmly, pushing the boiling anger back down again. "I do. And I need to confront my father. We're gonna have a come-to-Jesus moment, him and I."

He took a right and began bouncing down the washboard road towards the trailhead. "Someday, the county is going to fix these roads," he yelled over the clatter. He was sure half of the noise was coming from just his teeth alone, chattering from the ruts on the awful road.

Georgia nodded and smiled, but didn't try to shout anything over the noise. Moose held on tight to the steering wheel, all of his attention required just to keep his truck on the road. More than anything else, this calmed him down. Focusing on something other than the overwhelming anger and hurt and betrayal welling up inside of him helped his racing heart finally start to slow.

A little of the anger faded away, replaced by determination. A determination to take his life into his own hands.

Finally, they pulled to a stop into the parking lot next to her car, and the quiet in the truck was almost deafening.

"Well, I better—" Georgia said, reaching for the door handle just as Moose blurted out, "Will you go out with me?"

Time stood still as Georgia spun in her seat, staring up at him. "What?" she breathed.

"Will you go out with me?" he asked again, this time more confident. It's what he wanted, and it's what she wanted. He was *sure* of it.

And yet, she shook her head.

"I can't," she whispered, her eyes dark with pain. "You know that. Tenny is my cousin; the sister I never got to have. We're really different in a lot of ways, but she's still one of my closest friends."

He drew in a deep breath. She was right. Of course. He couldn't just skip from one cousin to the next. He should branch out of the Rowland Family Tree. Maybe try dating someone from Franklin. That'd be different.

Hell, considering he'd spent his whole life dating one girl, just about anything would be different.

"Then, once you've talked to Tennessee, come talk to me," she finished. "We can discuss…things from there." She reached out and stroked his cheek, her fingers sliding over the rough stubble he hadn't taken the time to shave off that morning, and then she was gone, grabbing her purse and jumping from the truck, sliding into her car and slamming the door closed behind her. She took off out of the small dirt parking lot before Moose could even shake himself from the stupor her touch had cast over him.

Tennessee…

Georgia was right. He had to take care of one disaster before even attempting to start another.

But, Georgia wanted to talk to him after he told Tennessee the truth, and that gave him a bit of hope. She wouldn't say that if she didn't see a future with him, right?

Before he got to discover the answer to that question, though, he had to break Tennessee's heart, a thought that made his own heart twist a little. It wasn't what he wanted. It'd never been what he wanted.

It was what he was going to do, though. Because marrying her when he didn't love her would hurt her even more.

Maybe it was the selfishness of his own desire to be free of her and the obligation she represented that made him think that. Maybe he was pretending he was doing the noble thing here because facing the truth – that he wasn't strong enough to do what duty called for, no matter what his heart wanted – was too damn painful.

But Tennessee, her father, his father…they all needed to know the truth. Then he'd be free for the first time in his life.

You're going to lose the dealership.

The thought came out of nowhere, a lightning strike out of a bright blue sky. All the more jolting and painful because of that, and because…well, it was probably true.

He leaned back, banging his head against the headrest.

He was going to lose the dealership. Dammit to hell and back, his father would never put up with this rebellion.

But honestly, who would he give it to? Rhys? Moose's younger brother was in Japan, after having run away from their father by joining the Navy as soon as he graduated from high school. He would die before being stuck in Sawyer, Idaho, working at the John Deere dealership.

Zara? First off, she was a girl, and his father was too much of a male chauvinistic pig to let his daughter inherit the dealership. Second, she wanted to become a doctor. She'd told Moose more than once that she was going to run the Long Valley County Hospital someday. She didn't want the Garrett Tractor & Implement Dealership any more than Rhys did.

Hell, his father would probably just decide that he'd live forever, and then he wouldn't have to pass the dealership on to anyone at all. Not only would that seem reasonable to him, he'd make it happen out of sheer force of will.

Moose had a lot of thinking to do. He headed back down the washboard road, but instead of taking a left back towards town, he decided to take a right and head further into the hills. Maybe it was time to have a come-to-Jesus talk…with himself.

CHAPTER 14
GEORGIA

GEORGIA STOOD UP from her desk with a big stretch and groan. After her adventure up in the hills, her body was still recuperating and she found that there were parts of her that ached that she didn't even realize existed.

She looked down at her oversized desk with pride. She'd managed to get the report on car loan defaults done and into the main branch just minutes before the deadline, and had even started the process on a new vehicle loan for Abby and Wyatt Miller. They were filling out the paperwork to bring another foster child home and had come to the realization that a truck, even a quad-cab, wasn't big enough. They were on the hunt for an SUV so they could cart their soon-to-be growing brood around with them.

It was still a little weird, honestly, to see Wyatt smiling and holding hands with Abby, completely in love with his new wife. They'd brought Juan – their foster son – in with them, and had proudly talked about being close to finishing the adoption process. Juan hadn't said a word, but had beamed from ear to ear, clearly as thrilled about life as his soon-to-be parents.

Seeing Wyatt happy…it helped Georgia realize what Abby

had seen in him in the first place. When she'd first heard that Abby was dating Wyatt, she was sure her friend had gone insane. Grumpy, testy, snappy, asshole-ly Wyatt Miller? Why on God's green earth would Abby want to date *him*? He was handsome and all, but not *that* handsome – not handsome enough to put up with that kind of personality.

No one in town had seen his soft and caring underbelly, until Abby had brought it out in him, and shown it to the world. Georgia had even heard that Stetson and Wyatt were honest-to-God friends now, which Georgia would've bet her right arm would never happen. They'd been at each other's throats their whole lives.

Transformations like this didn't happen every day, that was for damn sure.

Tripp knocked on her office door while sticking his head through and looking at her. "Hey, you've got a reporter here…?" he said, a question more than a statement. *What do you want me to tell them?* was written clearly in his eyes.

Georgia looked back quizzically, trying to think why a reporter would want to talk to her. Her donation to the fundraiser for the fire department? That'd been a week ago. It seemed a little late to be writing that story, but she couldn't think of anything else even remotely possible. "Tell 'em to come in," she finally said. Standing around and wondering why a reporter was there certainly wouldn't get her the answers she wanted.

In came a taller woman, high heels causing her to tower over Georgia as she stuck her hand out to shake. "Hi, I'm Penny Roth," she said with a knuckle-cracking handshake. "Mr. Toewes sent me down here to interview you for a story that'll run in both the *Times* and *Gazette*. You were out in that fire in the foothills a couple of days ago?"

Oh. Right. That made a hell of a lot more sense than them choosing to focus on the fire department fundraiser. They were sister papers, with the *Gazette* covering Franklin and the *Times* covering Sawyer. It was flattering, if awkward as hell, to think that someone would want to interview her, though.

Sawyer Times had interviewed her only once before, back when she'd just been promoted to branch manager at the credit union, and once in a lifetime was enough for her.

"I…I was," Georgia said hesitantly. *How to gracefully get out of this interview…*

And then, inspiration struck. "You know, what you should do is a piece on the Sawyer Fire Department as a whole. They did a big fundraiser a week ago that you could ask them about, and after all, it was one of their firefighters who saved me from that fire. All I did was live through it by hunkering down."

She shrugged, feeling pinned to the carpet by the reporter's intense gaze. "These men are the ones who put their lives on the line to save others. There's a training meeting tonight at 6:30 at the fire department. Why don't you swing by there? I'll stop by, too. Then you can interview all of us at the same time."

"That's a brilliant suggestion!" Penny said, her eyes sparkling at the idea, her bright red lips curling into a wide smile. "Thank you! I'll tell Mr. Toewes that I'll follow up on this tonight. See you then." She headed out with a swish of her skirts, closing the door quietly behind her.

Georgia stared at the door, feeling a bit like she'd just lived through a human-sized tornado.

At least tonight at the fire station, she'd have the other guys there to help her manage the sheer amount of energy that radiated off Penny the Reporter with every step.

Now that she'd voluntold the department for a group interview, she should probably warn them about it. She picked up the phone, biting her lower lip with worry. Hopefully none of the men were *too* camera shy…well, other than Troy, of course. He didn't even speak to his fellow firefighters; he certainly wasn't going to open up to a newspaper reporter, of all people.

Well, there was no getting out of it now. If they wanted to hate on her for voluntelling them for this, so be it.

She dialed the number for the fire station.

CHAPTER 15

MOOSE

Moose pulled up in front of the fire station, his stomach dancing with nerves. Jaxson had sent out the call earlier, telling everyone what to expect that night at their monthly training session, so Moose'd actually taken the time to put on a nice pearl-snap shirt and hole-free Wranglers instead of just showing up in his greasy John Deere uniform like he normally would.

It wasn't the newspaper reporter coming that was making him nervous, although it was awkward to think that someone wanted to interview him. That was the sort of thing that his father did, not Moose.

No, it was more the small matter of Georgia being here tonight; he hadn't had the time to talk to his dad or Tennessee yet, so he couldn't walk right up to her and lay one on her like he so desperately wanted.

On top of that, just being around her made his hair stand on end, like he'd accidentally touched a live wire while standing in a puddle of water.

The thought made him chuckle to himself. Honestly, his hair wasn't the only thing that stood at attention around her…

Somehow, by a miracle of the universe, his father hadn't

heard about him sneaking out early to go drive Georgia out to her car, and so when Moose had finally gotten home last night, ready for a big fight, he'd discovered it was just a normal evening in the Garrett household. Zara had been watching TV while playing on her phone; his mom had been loading up the dishwasher; his dad had been tinkering out in the garage on an old John Deere tractor he was in the middle of restoring.

Moose wasn't sure if he was happy for the reprieve, or disgruntled that it would continue to hang over him, worrying at him. Sure, he could choose to confront his dad right now, but why? He should let the peace linger just a day or two more. Be totally sure of what he wanted to say, *then* approach him.

He absolutely wasn't a wimp.

Absolutely.

He blinked, focusing on the world around him. He realized he was still hiding out in his truck and forced himself to get out. He couldn't spend the whole evening hunkered down in it; hiding from the questions in Georgia's eyes. He headed for the open bay, the hard fluorescent light spilling out into the cool early summer evening, when he saw Georgia's car pull into the gravel parking lot, tires crunching to a stop next to his truck.

The butterflies kicked up another notch.

Manners dictated that he help her out of her car, not just stand around like a nervous 15-year-old boy on his first date, and so he hurried to the driver's side door, opening it and extending his hand out to her.

"Hi," he said softly, his eyes taking in her skirt and blouse, paired with towering high heels. Taking his hand, she slid out of the car and to her feet in one graceful move. She looked up at him – no, she looked *at* him. With her high heels on, they were almost the same height. It was a little strange how off this felt to be practically eye to eye with her.

She smiled, a beautiful smile that threw him for a loop, and asked, "How are you?"

Was she breathless? She sounded a little…breathy to him.

Was she asking in code if he'd talked to Tennessee or his father yet? He couldn't tell.

"Good," he said smoothly, his voice sounding even and unperturbed. "Ready to head inside?"

She nodded, her curled blonde hair glinting in the harsh light streaming from the open bay, and then they were walking side by side, as if nothing at all was amiss.

As if he hadn't swallowed boiling lava.

Inside, the volunteer firefighters were milling around – Luke Nash and his hired hand Dylan along with Levi and Jaxson, with Troy sitting off to the side, idly petting Sparky who was leaning contentedly up against his legs. Levi looked up with a smile on his face, a smile that quickly faded when he saw Moose and Georgia walk in together.

They hadn't been touching; they hadn't even been talking.

But Levi was pissed anyway.

Instinctually they split, with Georgia heading over to pet Sparky and ask Troy how she was doing, while Moose headed towards the knot of men, all talking and laughing. All of them except for Levi, of course.

Moose came to a stop next to his best friend, who was rigid, a muscle ticking in his jaw. The conversation flowed around them as Moose tried to think of what to say.

"There's nothing between us," wasn't true. "We weren't doing anything," was true but defensive-sounding. "If you were going to make a move on her, you should've done it a long time ago," was aggressive and mean. Levi was his favorite person in the world. He couldn't say something so abrasive to him, even if it was true.

And anyway, Levi *had* made his move on her. They'd dated for years. And then, when he'd asked her to marry him, she'd turned him down flat.

She didn't want kids; he did.

There wasn't a whole lot of middle ground between the two points of view, and just like that, they were finished as a couple.

Dad would shit a brick if I not only married the wrong cousin, but refused to give him grandchildren.

Moose smiled a little to himself, the thought giving him a perverse bolt of pleasure. Revenge for everything his father had put him through would be bittersweet, though, because Moose wanted children. Giving them up for Georgia…

That would be the biggest sacrifice of all. Even bigger than losing the dealership.

Am I willing to lose everything, just to gain the chance at a relationship with a woman I've never even kissed?

On the surface, the idea seemed insane – downright stupid, really – but even as he told himself that, he couldn't convince his soul of its truth. Georgia just felt right, like a key sliding into a lock. He craved that feeling more than—

The air changed suddenly and Moose looked up, spotting a tall, gorgeous woman walking through the open bay door, a large, friendly smile gracing her lips. She walked with a natural sway to her hips, oozing womanhood and pure sex appeal with every step.

Ohhhhh…

This. This was why Georgia had spent so much time getting dolled up for tonight. She was nervous about her competition.

Moose wanted to snort with laughter even as he turned to find Georgia in the open bay area. The idea of some woman outshining Georgia was ridiculous on the face of it. No one was prettier. No one was funnier. No one was more perfect.

He caught her gaze and winked, and even in the dim lighting, he saw the blush covering her cheeks.

She liked him enough to fight for him, using a skirt, make-up, and high heels that made her legs look like they went on forever.

A grin spread across his face. He felt ten feet tall.

The newspaper reporter – Penny was her name, turned out – was going around the grimy bay, introducing herself and scribbling notes down on a pad as she went. She stopped in front of Sparky and Troy, Georgia standing awkwardly to the side as Penny introduced herself to Troy, kneeling to pet and love on Sparky.

"Aren't you a sweetie," she cooed, letting Sparky give her face a bath while her tail swept up a storm on the dusty cement floor. Moose was shocked to see it; somehow, this elegant woman didn't seem like the kind to kneel on a dirty concrete floor, and certainly didn't seem like the kind to inspire a deep and abiding love in a dog.

But Sparky seemed to love Penny on sight almost as much as she loved Troy.

Interesting…

He walked over to stand casually next to Georgia. He wanted to observe this up close and personal.

"So you're the one who saved Georgia from the fire?" the reporter asked, looking up at Troy, obvious interest in her eyes. Troy was perched on the tailgate of the water truck, Sparky tucked between his legs, the close proximity of the reporter seeming to unsettle the usually rock-solid man.

"No, not me," Troy said, shaking his head. He jerked his head towards Moose. "He did."

"I thought the dog was found up in the fire," Penny said, her brow knotted with confusion. "How did she end up with you, then?"

"She likes me," Troy said simply, shrugging his shoulders.

Moose couldn't believe his eyes. Or his ears, actually. Although these would seem like terse answers to most of humanity, he knew Troy well enough to know that he was practically spouting speeches at this point. So many words at the same time…

Why, he was being downright loquacious.

"How long have you been a firefighter?" she asked, continuing to pet Sparky as she looked at Troy, ignoring the whole supposed reason for her being there – Moose and Georgia.

Moose felt Georgia moving and he looked over to see her shoulders shaking with suppressed mirth. They caught gazes and grinned at each other. All jealousy was gone, and for just a quick moment, Moose missed it. It was kinda nice to be desired like that.

They stood there for a minute more, listening as the reporter asked probing questions and Troy gave short, to-the-point answers, appearing to be alternating between excitement to be the center of this woman's attention…and sheer terror.

After a bit, though, it started to feel like they were a third wheel on a blind date, and they instinctively moved back towards the knot of men Moose had left behind, no words needing to be exchanged between them.

"How's the interview going?" Jaxson asked, a huge grin on his face as he peered over their shoulders at the two – no, three, counting Sparky – of them in the corner. "Answering lots of questions?"

"Someone is," Moose said with a laugh.

They stood around for a minute longer, and then Jaxson shrugged his shoulders. "I'd like to get going so I can head back home at a decent hour," he said. "If she thinks of any questions for the rest of us, we can answer them then. In the meanwhile, let's get started on our training. Tonight, I thought we'd talk about how to detect—"

Moose turned to Georgia, who was worrying her bottom lip as she listened to Jaxson talk. She was clearly debating – should she stay? Should she go? She didn't want to be a third wheel on the pseudo-date happening in the corner, but she also wasn't a member of the Sawyer Fire Department.

"You should go hang out at the desk," Moose whispered, jerking his head towards the paperwork desk, where overstuffed cubbies held every form the fire department could ever need, and some outdated ones too that no one'd ever bothered to throw away. "Just for a few more minutes. Just in case."

She paused for a moment and then nodded, heading for the desk, her skirt tight across her ass, her heels showing off every slender curve of her calves. Moose suddenly had a hard time breathing. The newspaper reporter was pretty, sure, but she was no Georgia.

He looked over and saw Levi's stormy face. He'd obviously caught the whole exchange. Moose sucked in a quick breath, feeling like he'd been punched in the stomach. He needed to talk to his best friend, and soon – before his best friend refused to talk back.

CHAPTER 16

GEORGIA

GEORGIA SLID INTO HER car and shoved the key into the ignition, but didn't turn it. Instead, she folded her arms across the top of the steering wheel and dropped her head with a thunk.

Seeing Moose tonight had been exquisite torture. He hadn't talked to Tennessee or his father yet, of that she was sure. She knew she would've heard the explosions all the way over at her condo if he had. She couldn't figure out what was taking so long. Sure, it'd only been 24 hours, but it was the longest 24 hours of her life.

Did he not actually want to break things off with her cousin? Was Georgia somehow the other woman?

She groaned, beating her head against her folded arms repeatedly. If someone didn't talk, and soon, she was going to go stark-raving mad. Did no one realize how hard it was to keep her hands to herself? To not kiss and touch and curl up against Moose?

Not to mention that she wanted Moose and Tennessee officially over with for her cousin's sake. She couldn't break Tenny's confidence in her; she couldn't tell Moose what Tennessee refused to say. She'd given her cousin her word that night at the fundraiser, and she couldn't break it now, no matter how much her soul begged her to.

But if talking didn't start soon, she was going to drag everyone into a room and lock them in there until the air was cleared.

The idea was starting to sound better by the moment, honestly.

She finally started her car and pulled out of the parking lot. It was time to go home and drink a glass of wine. Or three. She could curl up with a Tessa Dare book, and pretend for a moment that her own life would be fixed and going along swimmingly if she just made it through the next three chapters.

If only real life were like a romance novel. She could use a little bit of happily ever after right about now.

CHAPTER 17

MOOSE

MOOSE STOOD on the front doorstep of the imposing Rowland family home, shifting from cowboy boot to cowboy boot. He had the requisite bouquet of flowers in a stranglehold in front of him, clinging to them as if to a life preserver. He'd brought yellow roses over tonight instead of the usual red; yellow meant friendship. Red meant love. Even he knew that.

So, yellow it was.

Gathering his courage, he knocked firmly on the front door of the Georgian plantation home – or the closest replica to be found this side of the Mississippi. The style seemed horribly out of place up in the wilds of Idaho, but it's what Tennessee's parents considered to be the best.

And they *always* had to have the best.

Tennessee's mother opened the door, a haughty look on her face that melted into a smile once she spotted him. "Oh, hi dear!" she exclaimed, standing back to welcome him inside. "Come in, come in. We didn't realize we would be graced by your presence this evening. What a lovely surprise. Tennessee!" she called up the grand staircase. "Deere is here to see you."

Moose kept a smile firmly planted on his face even as he

fought back the urge to correct her usage of his legal name. He was Moose…to everyone he cared about.

In that case, he figured that maybe it wasn't so bad to be called "Deere" by Tennessee's mom after all. He felt a lot of things at that moment, but genuine love for the pretentious, snotty woman standing in front of him was *not* one of those feelings.

Tennessee peered down over the railing, her hair falling forward in a riot of curls as she tried to see who was in the foyer. "Oh, hi Deere!" she said, the surprise evident in her voice. She had on a pair of yoga pants and a sweatshirt. "Please…I'll be right down. Mother, can you take him to the drawing room?" She disappeared from sight, probably to change into something more formal.

He wanted to tell her not to bother (it wasn't nice to have her get all dressed up just so he could break her heart) but he also didn't know how to holler that up the stairs (that wasn't exactly the sort of thing you *could* holler up the stairs) and so he just allowed her mother to lead him to the drawing room, as if he didn't know *exactly* where it was. It was where he was directed every time he came over to visit Tennessee, as if he was the lead character in some dreadful Regency novel. No doubt Tennessee's parents felt like they'd been born into the wrong century *and* country. They certainly acted like that, anyway.

"She'll be right down," Tennessee's mother promised him, and then shut the French doors to the drawing room behind her, leaving him in the dim lighting of just one lamp glowing in the corner.

He wandered over to the grand piano and plunked at a few keys, the rich sound belying his complete ineptitude. No wonder Tennessee sounded so amazing when she played the piano. A three year old would sound amazing banging on these keys.

Not that Tennessee didn't have musical talent – she did – but there was no denying that this piano was worth some serious cash.

Only the best for the Rowland family…

"Hi, Moose!" Tennessee said, slipping into the drawing room and closing the door with a *click* behind her. She was wearing a calf-length bright blue dress that matched the color of her eyes perfectly, with her hair up in a stunning cascade of curls that tumbled over her shoulder. She looked like she was ready for an evening out at an upscale restaurant and an opera to finish off the date.

Moose felt his stomach begin to clench harder. If he threw up, he would never live it down. He'd have to move to Timbuktu and change his name to John Smith.

Just tell her the truth…just tell her the truth…

"Oh look, you brought me roses. Yellow ones, even. Usually you bring me red ones!" she said delightedly. She took the roses from his sweaty grasp, leaving him with nothing to cling to. He swallowed down the desire to ask her to give them back, please, and instead shot her a devil-may-care grin.

"I thought it was a nice change of pace," he said with a shrug.

"Yellow roses are my favorite!" she said with a huge smile, burying her face in their petals. "Red are fine, of course," she said quickly. "I love them too. I just…yellow is so cheerful, you know?"

She was obviously worried about offending him, which made a bubble of hysterical laughter attempt to work its way up his throat. He'd been sort of dating / engaged to / connected with Tennessee his entire life, and he'd had no idea that yellow roses were her favorite.

What had they been thinking?

"I cannot marry you," he blurted out, and then all color drained from his face. It was what he'd been thinking, but he hadn't meant to actually say it. He'd meant to break it to her gently, after reassuring her about how beautiful she was, and how lucky any man would be to marry her. He just didn't happen to be that man. She shouldn't take it personally, of course.

Yada yada yada.

But then…the words just flew out of his mouth, like a dog spotting an opening in the fence and making a run for it.

"Wh-what?" she stuttered, blue eyes huge as she looked at him over the bouquet of roses. "You don't want to marry me?"

"I should've told you a long time ago," he said, his heart breaking at the look in her eye. She was completely stunned by this. Of *course* she was stunned by this. What, did he expect her to be excited about it? He hurried on before she could curse his name or knee him in the nuts or any other number of things he absolutely deserved. "I'm sorry. I should've told you. I…I don't love you, Tennessee. You're beautiful and talented and intelligent and kind, and you're going to make someone a smashing wife someday. I just can't be—"

"Oh *thank you*!" she hollered, throwing herself at him, covering his face in kisses. She was laughing and crying as she hugged his neck tight. "Thank you, thank you, thank you."

He stiffened up, instinctively hugging her back even as the panic began to grow ever more out of control in the pit of his stomach, something that would've seemed impossible five minutes ago but was now proving to be quite possible.

"I…I *don't* want to marry you," Moose felt obliged to point out. Somewhere, the lines had been crossed. She was going to be pissed when she realized what he really said. She might even knee him in the nuts twice for good measure. She somehow got the impression that he was finally proposing to her.

No, no, no, no…this is not *good!*

"Tennessee," he said urgently, clasping her hands in his, the giant bouquet of roses keeping them a good foot apart from each other, "I *can't* marry you."

"And I can't marry you!" she announced, a huge grin on her face. "Nothing personal, of course. But I cannot marry my brother. You've always been there, like the coffee table or something—" His mind spun at that, his ego a little bruised at the comparison. Coffee table? Couldn't she have picked something better? Something not…furniture related? "—and I just kept thinking that it was making you and Dad and Mom happy, so I had to do it anyway, but I don't love you. I've never loved you."

"Never…loved me?" He repeated her comment, stunned, his mind whirling like a child's toy as he tried to take it in. This whole conversation was blowing his mind. If Tennessee had loudly announced that she was actually a transvestite and was going to move to New York to start a one-person nudist play, he could not have been more shocked.

"Nope!" she said with a huge grin. "Never. I mean, like a brother, sure. But not like I should love my future *husband*."

"Uh-huh," he said faintly, feeling his way to the couch and sitting down with a thud. He'd spent *years* of his life subconsciously trying to work his way up to this moment, and had spent the last 48 hours of his life trying to imagine how she'd take the news.

This…this wasn't it. This wasn't what he'd imagined at all. She was smiling and laughing, not sobbing hysterically. This was just *wrong*.

"Are you okay?" she asked, pausing in her excited dancing to stare at him worriedly. "You did say you didn't want to marry me, right? And I don't want to marry you. I mean, we still have to tell the parents and God knows *that's* going to go over like a lead balloon, but you and I, we're on the same page, right?"

"Yes…" he breathed out, the news finally becoming real to him. "Yes, we are. I don't want to marry you, and you don't want to marry me!" He jumped up from the couch, a grin splitting his face from ear to ear as they danced and laughed, relief washing over them in waves. "I—I thought you were going to be heartbroken!" he sputtered, pulling back from yet another hug of happiness. "I've been worried about this for… well, for years, even if I didn't let myself really think about it, and…you're not angry! I was just sure you'd be mad at me!"

"Mad? That finally one of us has the backbone to say no to this? I'm thrilled beyond words. This is the best present you could've ever given me."

They grinned at each other for a minute, the elation washing over them as they both reveled in the feeling of freedom. It was a feeling they'd never really felt – never, in their whole lives – and it was intoxicating. Way better than the best whiskey money could buy.

He took her hand and dragged her back to the couch, pulling her down beside him. "Okay, planning time. We need to present a united front to our parents. I'm afraid that if they get us alone, they'll guilt us back into a relationship. Not to mention that apparently, my father was going to hold the dealership hostage until I married you."

"Wait, you didn't know that?" Tennessee asked, jerking her head back in surprise.

"Of course I didn't know that. How messed up is that?! Forcing your child to marry the woman of your choice before you'll finally hand over the reins to a business you've been promising that child his entire life? Hell, what century do we live in, anyway?"

She let out a little giggle at that, which quickly escalated into a belly laugh. "I don't knoooow!" she said, weak from the laughter as she collapsed against the corner of the couch, tears streaming down her face. "I know we live in Sawyer, Idaho of all places, but it is 2018, right? We shouldn't be a few centuries behind the times, right?"

"You wouldn't think so, but…" Moose trailed off, wonder in his voice as he watched Tennessee let go, sprawling loose-limbed over the couch beside him. In all the years he'd known her, he'd never seen her laugh like this. He didn't know she even knew how to laugh like this.

He didn't know she didn't want to marry him. He didn't know her favorite flower was the yellow rose. He didn't know she knew how to let out an old-fashioned belly laugh.

He didn't know her at all.

He'd thought his heart would be hurting as they had an ultra-serious discussion and she cried and yelled and beat him over the head with her shoe. Instead, his head was hurting as he tried to wrap his mind around the fact that he could know a woman his entire life, and yet, know nothing about her at all.

"You are the most private person I know," he blurted out. "How is it that I didn't really know you?"

She sucked in a quick breath, the humor instantly gone. She sat up, wiping away the tears of laughter from her eyes with the backs of her hands, and then whispered, "Honestly, you probably know me better than almost anyone else."

She took in a deep breath and he could tell that she was really thinking about what she was going to say, making sure she said precisely what she meant.

"I...I was taught a long time ago that what I want and think and desire doesn't really matter, so why share it?" She shrugged. "Virginia is in her own little world while my parents don't care what I want, so that leaves you and Georgia. I guess I just got into the mindset that it really didn't matter what I thought, so I would just bury it down deep. Better than trying to share and being told to my face that I didn't matter."

Her eyes were glistening with tears, and he realized belatedly that the euphoria had dissipated. Now the real challenge was just beginning: What on earth was he going to tell her parents? His parents? This wasn't just going to cause a little bit of frustration and anger, it was going to throw off the whole balance of the universe.

The tears began rolling down Tennessee's face, and instinctively, he pulled her head against his chest, stroking her head as she cried out years of anger and callousness and ignorance of who she really was by a set of parents who really didn't care.

As hard as it was to see her cry like this, Moose also realized that it was cathartic. She deserved to just let it all out.

Before he could say anything – if there was anything *to* say in a situation like this – the door to the drawing room opened. "What on earth is going on in here?" Mrs. Rowland demanded, hurrying over and staring down at the two of them on the couch together. "Tennessee, quit your crying. No one wants to see your red eyes. They're not at all attractive. First you two were laughing like a pair of loons, and now you're crying. Deere, explain yourself. What did you say to Tennessee?"

He opened his mouth to defend himself, when Tennessee spoke up. "Mother," she said, sitting up and again wiping at the tears on her cheeks with the backs of her hands. This time, though, they were not tears of joy and the gesture hurt Moose to watch, sending a pain shooting through his gut at the sight. Tennessee wasn't one to cry easily. How they'd ever found themselves in this situation was painful to contemplate. "We have a big announcement to make. Can you go get Father out of the den? This is important."

Mrs. Rowland's eyes flicked back and forth between them, clearly trying to decide whether she could bully Tennessee into telling her now, but Moose draped his arm around Tennessee's shoulders and looked up at the woman with a bland look on his face. He wasn't going to move an inch until they got what they wanted.

"Well, I'm sure your father wants to hear whatever it is you have to say," Mrs. Rowland finally sniffed, and headed out the door to hunt him down. As soon as she left, Virginia slipped in through the partially open door and hurried over.

"What is going on?" she whispered, her eyes darting between the two of them. "Laughing and shouting and crying… I thought Mother was going to go crazy, pacing back and forth at the door, trying to figure out what you two were doing."

"Come, sit next to me," Tennessee said, patting the cushions next to her on the couch for her teenage sister to sit on. "You're about to witness your older sister actually using the backbone God gave her at birth. The fireworks should be...interesting."

"Are you two...are you breaking up?" Virginia whispered, her eyes round as they darted back and forth between the two of them. Tennessee paused for just a moment, debating, and then she nodded. Virginia flopped back on the couch.

"Shiiittttt," she said in awe.

And then, "Mother is gonna kill you."

"Probably. You can only stay and watch the show if you keep quiet, though," Tennessee warned her. "No comments from the peanut gallery."

Virginia mimed zipping her lips and throwing away the key, then settled down on the couch in a more proper position that wouldn't earn her a scolding from her mother. She took the threat of being thrown out seriously, and decided to stop talking before their parents even showed up. She didn't dare risk missing the show.

Moose stroked Tennessee's shoulders. He could feel the tension in her, vibrating as she tried to project an aura of calm. She looked up at him with a pained grimace on her face, patting him on the knee, trying to pretend as if all was well, and he let out a little chuckle. In that moment, he felt closer to her than he had in all of the years of "dating." He could practically read her thoughts as they marched across her face.

Maybe...maybe if I'd been able to see the "real" her all these years, I might've fallen in love with her.

Then Georgia's smiling face flashed in front of his eyes and he felt a little smile curl around his lips. Nope. There was no hope for Tennessee – never had been. Not with Georgia Rowland in the world.

"What are you grinning about?" Tennessee demanded, her voice barely a whisper. She was going to vibrate right off the couch with all of the nervous energy built up inside of her.

"Georgia's smile," he said simply.

"I knew it!" she crowed. "There was always something between you two. Like walking into—"

"Something between whom?" came her father's voice as he strode into the room, his polo shirt neatly tucked into his slacks, a glass of whiskey in his hand. He'd obviously been disturbed from his evening routine, and was not at all happy about it. His wife came trailing in behind him. He glanced over at Virginia, sitting so straight, she might as well have had a steel bar for a spine. "What are *you* doing here?" he asked, getting more annoyed by the moment.

Virginia opened her mouth – probably to apologize – when Tennessee jumped to her defense. "I asked her to stay. I thought it would be good to have the whole Rowland family here to hear this. Mother, Father…" She drew in a deep breath. "Moose and I do not love each other. We never have. I am not going to marry him, and he's not going to marry me."

Moose felt a little laugh bubble up at that statement – the first part rather made the second part obvious – but Tennessee was nervous, her usually unflappable, demure demeanor gone, along with any pretense that she was going to continue to bend over backwards for her parents.

"You're *what*?!" her mother cried, while at the same time, her father thundered, "Over my dead body!"

"Father, it is 2018. I will choose who I marry. Moose is not that person. End of story."

"Such a ridiculous nickname!" her mother broke in, sidetracked by her daughter's use of it in front of her. "I never understood why you'd choose that name over the one your parents chose for you."

"Funny," Moose drawled, "I always thought the name 'Deere' was ridiculous. I guess it's all in how you look at it. I also wouldn't name my children after states, so…" He shrugged.

"Well, I never!" Mrs. Rowland exclaimed, her cheeks

growing redder by the moment. "If this is the kind of impertinence you show your betters, I am *glad* my daughter won't agree to marry you."

"Whatever makes you sleep better at night," Moose said with another insolent shrug, suddenly feeling a thousand pounds lighter. He turned towards Tennessee, ignoring the shrieks and yelling of the parents, and the howls of laughter from Virginia. "I think I've done enough damage around this popsicle joint. I'll take on my parents by myself. I'm pretty sure that after tonight's performance, your parents won't want me back, no matter what business I'm inheriting. I think we're in the clear," he said with a grin, leaning forward and kissing her on the cheek.

"Thanks for everything," she whispered back conspiratorially. "And do tell me how things go with Georgia."

He nodded his acknowledgement to Tennessee, winked at Virginia, waved cheerfully to the parents who were matching shades of red, and then walked out of the drawing room. "Young man, come back here!" he heard Mr. Rowland holler, but he just kept walking.

Freedom was sweet, indeed.

CHAPTER 18

GEORGIA

"GEORGIA," Tripp said, not even bothering to knock before sticking his head through, "Mr. Garrett is here—"

"What have you done to my son?" Mr. Garrett demanded, pushing past Tripp, the door slamming into the wall behind it with a crash. Georgia's eyes widened as she took in the sight in front of her – Mr. Garrett looked like he was just this side of foaming at the mouth as he stomped over to her desk. He leaned on her desk, towering over her.

Even as her mind was skittering through the possibilities that this man's question presented – had Moose finally talked to his parents, then? Did he and Tenny officially break up? – she also realized what Mr. Garrett was trying to do: Intimidate her with his height. Moose had definitely gotten his build from his dad, not his mom, and add to that fact that Georgia was sitting in her office chair, not standing up…she practically had to lean back into the dentist-chair position just to look him in the eye.

Screw that.

She stood up, smoothly sliding her feet into her heels as she did so. She'd taken them off earlier in the day, using the cover of the desk to get away with it, but now she wanted every inch of height she could get with this man.

"I did nothing to your son," she said calmly, and then looked past the frothing man to Tripp in the doorway, his eyes wide as he was debating what to do. "Tripp, please close the door. I don't want the whole credit union to hear this." He moved to leave, and she said, "No, please stay. I'd like a witness in case this man gets violent."

"Violent?" Mr. Garrett sputtered. "You think I'd hit a *woman*?"

"Quite honestly, sir, I don't know what to believe about you," she said bluntly. "So I'd like the help if I need it."

"My son," Mr. Garrett snarled, obviously wanting to stay on topic, "came home last night and told me that he broke up with Tennessee. He's not going to marry her. Said it was your idea!"

"My idea? Really? Is that *exactly* what he said?" she asked calmly, a little hint of humor in her voice. "Moose is a grown man. Are you trying to say that I told him he ought to break up with Tennessee, and that he jumped right on that and did it without any thought for what he actually wants?"

"I didn't say that!" he roared. "Don't you twist my words around on me."

"I wasn't twisting them," she pointed out, "just making sure I understood them. So if he is a grown man and he did make the decision to break up with Tennessee, why are you in here yelling at me?"

"I'm not yelling!" he thundered, and then his face went an even deeper shade of red – almost purple – as the ridiculousness of that statement penetrated even his anger-befuddled brain. "The important thing is," he gritted out through clenched teeth, his mouth barely moving as he made an obvious – and painful – effort to bring his volume under control, "he was happy with Tennessee until *you* came along and mixed him all up. If you hadn't tempted him to look elsewhere—"

"Sir, I've always been here," she interrupted, not bothering to let him finish. That would afford him the kind of courtesy he did not deserve. "I did not move to Long Valley last week."

His mouth opened and closed once…twice…and then what he was *really* thinking came out. "You are the daughter of the younger son, without an acre to his name," he spat out. "I will not have my son marry the daughter of the high school biology teacher and the elementary school cafeteria worker!"

"How very elitist of you," she said dryly, staring him right in the eye as she talked. She didn't so much as blink. She wasn't going to let him know that he was rattling her.

She wasn't going to let him rattle her, period.

"So my self worth is only based on my parents' occupation?" she continued. "Strange idea to have, coming from a self-made man."

Tripp's gasp of astonishment was the only sound in the room as Mr. Garrett glared at her, nostrils flaring, trying to stare her down. She simply stared back, arms folded, waiting for him to either continue to spar with her, or leave.

She wasn't going to move an inch.

Finally, he cracked and spoke first. "I've worked hard so my children wouldn't have to – so they could lead an easy life! Not one where they're trapped into a relationship with a gold digger."

Georgia's mind spun, trying to figure out where to even begin unpacking such a ridiculous statement. Moose led an easy life? His father ought to inform Moose of this fact; he'd be tickled pink to hear it. He regularly worked 18-hour days at the dealership. Maybe he'd be allowed to cut it back to only 12-hour shifts instead, now that he knew he was living the easy life.

And trapped? She was trapping Moose into a relationship? Did Mr. Garrett think she was pregnant or something? She and Moose hadn't even kissed. She wanted to burst out laughing at the absurdity of it all.

But she finally settled on responding to the last part of it. "Gold digger? How is it that you think I am a gold digger? I am the one who owns my own home. I own a brand-new car – paid for with cash. I have a nice insurance and retirement package through the credit union. Your son, meanwhile, still lives in his parents' basement, he drives a truck older than he is that's held together with duct tape and bailing wire, and I'm going to guess he has no retirement package to speak of. Exactly what gold am I digging here?"

"You want to marry him because then all of the farmers will get their John Deere tractor and operating loans through you!" he said triumphantly. "If you could wrap up all of the farming business in the valley, I bet that'd mean quite the Christmas bonus!"

"You think that Moose broke things off with Tennessee because I wanted a *Christmas* bonus? Sir, I do hope you realize how ridiculous you're sounding right now."

He tried to break in but she steamrolled right over him.

She was done being polite.

"I'm only going to say this once because it's quite frankly none of your business, but your son and I have yet to even kiss. If he's chosen to break up with Tennessee, that is his choice. If you think he's doing it to rebel against you as some sort of punishment for being a downright *awful* father, well…have you ever considered that maybe you should try being a better one? If your son is forced to rebel against you because you are an asshole, coming in here and yelling at *me* won't change that fact."

"You two haven't even kissed?" he hissed, ignoring the rest of her little speech as if she'd said nothing at all. "He made it sound like he was going to propose to you next week! Like he was madly in love with you!"

"I can only hope that's true," Georgia said with a nonchalance that she definitely didn't feel. What she wanted to do was a quick jig around the office. *Moose likes me – he really,*

really likes me! "He's obviously shared more with you than he has with me."

A smirk curled up around the edges of Mr. Garrett's mouth. "This is just puppy love," he spat out. "He's wanting to sow his oats a little before settling down with the *right* Rowland cousin. I mean, look at you. Would he honestly pick you over Tennessee in the end? You are the ugly cousin – everyone knows that. My son would never be so stupid."

She sucked in a breath between her teeth – a hiss of sound in the otherwise silent office. "Get out, Mr. Garrett," she said softly. "Your welcome has been overstayed. If you want to conduct business with the credit union in the future, you are to deal with my assistant manager. You are not to come in my office again. Tripp?"

She looked at her assistant manager who eagerly grabbed Mr. Garrett's elbow to escort him out the door.

"What are you doing!" he yelled, yanking his elbow away. "You cannot throw me out. I am Rocky Garr—"

"I am well aware of your name, Mr. Garrett," Georgia said smoothly. "Now leave."

"Or what? You'll call the cops on me?"

"Now that's an excellent idea," she said, reaching for her phone on her desk. "Why don't I just call Sheriff Connelly right now and he can come on down to escort you off the premises."

"Connelly would never arrest me," Mr. Garrett said triumphantly. "Not if he wants to get elected as sheriff again next year."

"Maybe not, but I'll make sure to discuss the situation loudly in the lobby of the bank," she said cooly. "I imagine the gossip chain here in Long Valley would chew over that one for a long time."

He hesitated, his whole body frozen as he tried to decide if she was serious; if it was worth it; if she'd really do something like that.

She picked up the phone from the cradle and began punching in the number for the sheriff's department.

"I'm done talking to a skank like you anyway," Mr. Garrett said coldly. "If my son does marry you, I'll cut him off without a penny. Think about what *that* will do to your future career. Any farmer who takes out a loan from you will pay higher than retail price from me at the dealership; I'll make sure of it."

He spun on his heel, pushing past Tripp and storming out into the lobby of the credit union, cursing as he went. There were a few startled yelps, which Georgia was pretty sure meant that he was shoving customers out of his way, and then the bell over the front glass doors jingled and he was gone.

She slowly hung up the phone.

"Heaven help you if you do marry Moose," Tripp said, staring at her with concern in his whiskey brown eyes. "Mr. Garrett had always been so nice when he came in before. I had no idea he could be like that…"

Georgia collapsed into her chair, all of the steel gone from her spine. She felt boneless, worn out, run over, and thrown away. "It's okay for me to underwrite loans for his customers. It's okay for him to bank here. But it's *not* okay for me to marry his son. When I was up in heaven, picking out families, I just picked the wrong brother to be born to." She gave Tripp an ironic smile. "Stupid, stupid me."

"Next time, make better choices, will you?" he said, and then began laughing. "What century are we living in, anyway?"

"I have no idea…"

CHAPTER 19
MOOSE

Moose paced back and forth, wearing down a path in the lush carpet in his bedroom. When he'd come home last night from the Rowland's, his father had already heard the news and was *furious*. Apparently, Mrs. Rowland had called over to relay the news as soon as Moose had walked out the door.

Dad had laid into Moose, telling him how he was failing the Garrett family, he was making the wrong choice, blah blah blah, hardly letting Moose get a word in edgewise, and then…he'd suddenly gone quiet. Scarily quiet. He'd told Moose he needed a day to "get used to the idea," and that he would talk to him again the next evening.

Moose had been completely taken aback. Who was this man, and what had he done with his father? Rocky Garrett was not the kind of man to want to think through decisions cooly and logically before making pronouncements. He tended to be the shoot-first-ask-questions-later sort of guy…*if* he ever bothered to get around to asking questions. Moose finally stuttered out his agreement to this plan and had watched his father walk out of the room.

It had been over with…for the moment.

But now it'd been 24 hours, and it was time for The Talk. Moose had spent the whole day wanting to call Georgia – wanting to tell her what had happened – but had made himself hold back. He wanted a resolution when he went to Georgia. He wanted to be able to tell her that he and his father had worked it all out.

Honestly, he wanted to give Georgia good news, but dammit, if his father didn't come home soon, he wasn't sure if he'd be able to contain himself much longer. He'd settle for giving "I don't know what will happen" news, if it meant being able to talk to Georgia. More than possibly anything in the world, he wanted to just hold her, without guilt or worry or the vague feeling of cheating on Tennessee.

And then, he wanted to kiss her. Kiss her until they couldn't breathe, and then carry her over to…

His mind screeched to a halt. Where, exactly, was he going to carry her? He couldn't make love to her in his parents' house. He couldn't afford a hotel. It would all have to be done at her condo.

Which he was all for her making money and pursuing a career, but…could he really be a kept man? Could he handle living in her place, knowing that she was way out-earning him, at least until he took over the dealership?

If he even got to take over the dealership?

And that didn't take into consideration the fact that marrying Georgia meant giving up having children of his own. She'd been blunt as a 2x4 upside the head about not being willing to have children when Levi had proposed to her.

Was Moose willing to give that up?

He reached the end of his bedroom and spun on his heel to head back the other direction. He was going to wear a hole right through the carpet at this rate but sitting still in that moment? Not possible.

He'd always had a general idea that his future meant that he'd marry Tennessee and have 2.5 kids and a John Deere dealership to call his own, but choosing Georgia meant walking away from it all.

He was happy to walk away from Tennessee, of course, and taking away his father's ability to control his life through the dealership was sounding less and less like a hardship every passing moment, but kids?

Children of his own?

How much do I love Georgia?

Before he could even begin to answer such a life-altering question, the front door slammed open and Dad came clomping through it, his steps echoing and creaking in the ceiling above him. "Deere!" he thundered. "Get up here right now!"

Moose could be sure of one thing that his father hadn't spent his "thinking time" doing: A nice round of yoga and contemplation on how to become a better father.

Moose stomped up the stairs, getting more pissed with every step. All of the indecision he'd been trying to work through disappeared in a puff of air. Right here, right now, it was time to take on his father and win.

The first thing to change? He was done being called to the carpet like a child. He was 26 years old, for hell's sakes, not a 12-year-old boy who'd snitched the last of the ice cream.

"Rocky!" he heard his mother scolding. "Why are you yelling at Deere like that? There is no reason to raise your voice in this house."

"Then Deere and I are gonna have to take it outside," his dad snarled, just as Moose came walking into the room, "because I'm not going to play patty-cake with my son. Not when he has a whore chasing after him, trying to get him to throw his future away."

Moose heard his younger sister on the living room couch behind him suck in a breath at that. The room went dark around the edges as anger washed over him.

"Do not call Georgia a whore," Moose said deliberately, shaking with rage as he stared at his father. "Do. Not. Do it."

"Now you two," his mother said placatingly. "We just need to—"

"I only want what's best for this family," his dad said, ignoring his wife completely. "That's all I've ever done – what my family needed me to. You, though, are a selfish bastard who doesn't care about us. Georgia's father has no land, no influence, no money. Have you seen that house they live in? A little 1970s shoebox. You need to choose your family, or I'll make the choice for you."

"Everything you do is for this family?" Moose repeated, sputtering and laughing sarcastically as he said it. "You don't care about this family, and you sure as hell don't care about me."

"I've had to work hard so you could take over the business!" his father shouted, his face turning a deep red as he did so. "Just because I don't hand it to you free and clear when you've done nothing to earn it doesn't make me a bad father. In fact, it makes me a good one!"

"So working me into the ground, treating me like shit, and dictating who I marry before I get to take over the dealership is your way of being a good father? Just curious – do I ever get to vote and ask for a shitty one to replace you, then? Because I'm pretty sure no father out there could be worse than you. When, exactly, were you planning on telling me that I only got to inherit the dealership *after* I married Tennessee? You always told me it was five years, five years, five years. You never said a word about Tennessee being part and parcel to that. When were you planning on telling me the truth?"

"I knew you wouldn't be able to handle the truth!" his dad shot back. "Just because I know what's best for you, and am making sure that you're not throwing your life away over the ugly cousin doesn't mean I'm wrong."

"The ugly cousin?" Moose repeated, bewildered. "Hold on,

you think *Georgia* is the ugly cousin?" He started laughing uproariously. "Okay, now that's a good one," he snorted, slapping his knee with glee. It felt good to laugh. He needed to laugh just then.

"You cannot honestly think that Georgia is prettier than Tennessee!" his dad gasped, staring at his son in shock. "Georgia is a little mousy thing—"

"Just because Georgia doesn't wear ten pounds of makeup and spend seven hours curling her hair every day doesn't make her ugly, Dad. I honest to God have no idea what Tennessee looks like when she wakes up in the morning. She wears so much goop on her face and in her hair…it's not for me. And fake fingernails? What is up with those? Going every week to get her hair and nails done – Georgia doesn't do that because she actually has a full-time job. Tennessee's full-time job is to look pretty and play the piano. That isn't a job, Dad, that's the life of a southern belle."

"Tennessee looks like the future wife of the most important man in town," his father said acidly. "Unlike Georgia, she actually takes the time to present her best side to the world. There is no such thing as natural beauty, and Tennessee is smart enough to know that."

"I. Don't. Love. Tennessee. Do I need to hire a skywriter? If you saw it written in the clouds, would you believe me then?"

"What in the fiery depths of hell does love have to do with it?" his dad tossed back. "Love and marriage aren't even remotely related. Have her as your mistress after you get married – I don't care." His mother let out a keening cry of pain at that, bending at the waist, rocking and holding her arms tight against herself. His father continued, ignoring his wife. "If you don't marry her, I'll…I'll give the dealership to Rhys!" he said triumphantly.

Moose laughed sarcastically even as his heart was breaking for his mother. He wanted to rush to her side; hold her and stroke her hair and tell her it was all going to be okay. It was pulling her to pieces to have her oldest son and her husband fight like this, and Moose felt awful for his part in that pain, even if he couldn't stop it from happening.

He focused his eyes on his father. He was the villain here, and Moose had to keep his head in the game, no matter how hard it was to see his mother hurting.

"Rhys wouldn't take the dealership if you handed it to him on a silver platter," he said baldly. "He hates this town, and he hates you. Do you really think he felt a burning desire to join the military? He didn't want to – he told me that he'd had his fill of being ordered around with you as his father – but it was the only ticket out of this hellhole you've trapped us kids into. He's in Japan right now because it's the farthest base on the globe from Sawyer, Idaho that he could get sent to. Face it, Dad – you'll have to live forever if you're not going to give the dealership to me."

"Well…well, I don't have to make a decision about who I give it to for a long time," his dad snarled. "I have a lot of years left in me. Maybe Rhys will change his mind by then – who knows. All I know is, it won't be *you.*"

"Thank you for telling me that," Moose said with a smile he did not feel. "In that case, there is no reason left to stick around. I'll go pack my bags now. I'm not going to stay under the same roof as a man who thinks that dictating who I marry is the sign of a *good* father. Someday, you might realize how much you screwed this up. Or maybe not. But I won't sit around and wait for you to extract your head from your ass."

He spun on his heel and marched back down the stairs to the basement, the slow clap of Zara as she applauded his performance echoing down the stairs after him, intermingled with the cries of devastation from his mom. Zara's clapping wasn't exactly appropriate, but Moose couldn't help a quirk of his lips anyway. She was *such* a teenager sometimes. No wonder her and Virginia were best friends.

"Shut up!" his dad roared at his younger sister. The clapping stopped abruptly. Moose wanted to thunder back up the stairs to defend his sister and his mom; gather them up behind him and save them from the wrath of his father. But he knew even as he thought it that it would do no good at all. His mother had chosen a long time ago to stay with his father, despite his verbal abuse, and Zara was too young to move out. She would do it once she hit her 18th birthday though; he was willing to bet the dealership on that.

Ugh.

His heart squeezed a little at the unbidden thought, as he began throwing clothes and toiletries into his duffel bag. A saying he'd used his whole life – *I'd bet the dealership on that* – was no longer something he could say.

He couldn't bet what wasn't his.

He shoved the thought deep down, past the anger and hurt of his father's betrayal, so he didn't have to think about it or deal with it. If he buried it a mile down, so far down that no sunlight or moisture could ever get to it, then maybe he'd survive this mostly sane.

Maybe.

His mom knocked lightly on the open door, a Kleenex clutched in one hand. "Deere, you can't do this," she pleaded with him, dabbing at her eyes with the used Kleenex. "Your father is just upset right now. He doesn't know what he's saying. He will—"

"Your husband," Moose said pointedly, throwing his charge cords into his bag along with his beat-to-shit laptop, "knows exactly what he's saying and doing. He has worked his whole life to wrap me around his little finger and get me to jump as high as he wants me to jump, because he knew that I'd perform tricks for him in exchange for the dealership. No more, Mother. No more.

"People in this town think of me as a spoiled rich kid because my dad is the almighty Rocky Garrett. They probably think I'm still living at home because I don't want to grow up and face the world and pay my own bills. They don't realize that after all this time, my father is still paying me minimum wage. I've been working down at the dealership since I was ten years old – stocking shelves, making coffee, pushing a broom – and yet I am the lowest paid employee of the company. I don't deserve pay raises, because all of this work is 'sweat equity' and I'm paying for the dealership through my blood, sweat, and tears. I was never told I had to pay for it with my soul."

He zipped up the duffel bag and slung it over his shoulder, turning to look at his distraught mother. "If you ever want to leave your husband, let me know. I'll help you walk away. Nothing is worth this, Mom – not the vacations, not the fancy house, not the nice car in the garage."

"Is that why you think I stay?" she whispered, her eyes filling with tears yet again. "For a *car*?! I stay for you children, and because—"

"If you're staying because of me," he cut her off, not wanting to hear her proclaim her undying love to her bastard of a husband, "then you'll walk out that door with me right now."

"I can't leave," she protested. "Zara is upstairs. She needs me—"

"She needs you to show a backbone. She needs you to get her out of this hellhole. We can all walk out together, right here, right now."

"And go where?" his mom asked plaintively. "And do what? I have no marketable skills. I have no resumé. I cannot write down, 'I make beds and do laundry' on a job application."

"You can if you were applying to be a maid," Moose pointed out. At the shocked look on his mother's face, he let out a painful sigh. "I get it, Mom. It's scary out there for you. And it's scary for me. Dad just stole my future from me and I have no idea what I'm going to do with myself now. But I do know that I'm ready to go see what I can make of this world."

He hugged her hard, kissed her on the cheek, walked up the stairs, saluted his sister, ignored the man pouring himself a whiskey, and walked out the front door. For a second time in two days, he'd chosen freedom over security. The choice was scary as hell…

But it also felt like the most euphoric drug on the planet.

He was finally going to be his own person.

CHAPTER 20

GEORGIA

IT'D BEEN A WEEK since Moose's father had come storming into her office, yelling at the top of his lungs, and then… nothing. At first, Georgia had chalked it up to Moose needing to straighten out his relationship with his dad. They would talk to each other, figure things out, and then he could come by and talk to her.

Simple.

Except for the part where he wasn't coming by to talk to her.

The tiny insidious voice deep down inside of her that began as not even a whisper but rather a hint of a whisper on a breeze, began to grow louder.

Maybe Moose *had* chosen Tennessee after all. Maybe… maybe Moose had finally come to his senses and realized the truth that everyone else already knew: Georgia was the ugly cousin.

She wouldn't have put it as crudely as Mr. Garrett did, of course, but there was no denying he was right. Georgia had the kind of simple beauty that *didn't* stop men in the streets. *Didn't* leave their tongues hanging out of their mouths when they saw her.

She wasn't unfortunate, with a nose three times too big for her face and crossed eyes, but…

Well, she sure as hell wasn't Tennessee.

Moose'd had his entire life to realize that, though, so it seemed a little late to show up to that particular party.

So perhaps it was more than that – instead, it was the threat of being disinherited that had broken him.

It was a lot to give up on the *hope* of a relationship with her. She understood…intellectually.

It still broke her heart.

She went running after work each evening, pounding down the running path around the lake on the edge of town. She wanted the burn of her thigh muscles and lungs to remind her that she was still alive. She wanted the clarity of mind that came from pushing her body to the limit.

She wanted Moose.

It was the beginning of day nine that had her starting to question everything she thought she knew about Moose. Surely if he'd decided to stay with Tenny; if he'd decided to marry her and inherit the dealership and continue on the path his parents had laid out for him at birth, he would've told her about it.

Right?

Yet hour after hour when he didn't appear, she began to question that. Her hand moved a thousand times towards her phone, wanting to shoot him a text or an email or a smoke signal or *something*. Ask him what he was thinking and what he was doing and why was he leaving her hanging here like this?

She always stopped herself though, because she'd told him what needed to happen:

He needed to talk to Tennessee, and then he could come talk to her. He'd obviously done the first part of that equation. She wasn't going to force him to do the second part.

She thought about asking her mom to ask her sister-in-law about Tennessee and Moose, but pride, plain and simple, stopped her from even doing that. She wasn't going to beg her mother to talk to Robert or Roberta. It wasn't fair to her mom, who didn't like her brother- and sister-in-law any more than Georgia did, and anyway, Georgia didn't want to admit that she wanted to know that badly.

Moose will come talk to me when he's ready. When he's ready. When he's ready…

Day eleven came, and Georgia noticed a flyer hanging in the foyer of the credit union when she went to open up the front doors at 9 o'clock. It was the first wine tasting and art show of the season in Franklin and would be happening next Monday night – Memorial Day evening.

It could be a fun way to kick off the summer with Moo–with Tripp. She needed to do something more than run in circles every evening and file paperwork all day, and hey, Tripp could scout out a cutie or two to hit on. She could be his wingman. Help him pick a good one out.

Because I obviously have such good taste in people…

She pushed that thought away and instead went in search of Tripp. She found him back in the vault, putting away the paperwork from the opening routine. "Hey, are you busy Monday night?"

THEY PUSHED their way through the crowd, wine glasses in hand as they moseyed on down the main street of Franklin, checking out the paintings on display as they went. There were lots of abstracts and paintings of people's dogs to look over, and then, they found the motherlode.

Tripp's eyes lit up as he spotted Austin Bishop's face on an oil painting outside of Once Upon a Trinket. "I heard about this," Tripp said, laughing, to Georgia. "Ivy McLain, Iris' younger sister, started painting these when Austin broke up with her." He grabbed Georgia's hand and pulled her over to the arranged paintings.

The feeling of laughter quickly faded, though, as they took in the art in front of them.

"Wow," Georgia breathed. "I had no idea Ivy was so talented. These are amazing. No wonder Austin took her back." Everyone had heard by now about the…overblown nature of Ivy's stories about her success in California, but the paintings in front of them said all that Georgia needed to know: The people of California were blind as bats if they didn't recognize her talents.

They began browsing the paintings, Austin everywhere she turned, and Georgia began imagining Moose's face on all of these. Could she hire Ivy to do a painting of Moose? Without him knowing it? And then she could hide it underneath the bed and only pull it out at night?

Okay, I officially need to adopt a cat. Or seven. This is out of control.

Finally, they'd finished looking through every Austin painting in the bunch, and they began to wander further down the street. Georgia pulled her coat tighter around herself, shivering against the light evening breeze blowing through. They were on the cusp of summer, but it was still cold in the evenings up in the mountains, especially without Moose there to keep her warm—

Stop it. Just stop it.

But then, as if her thoughts had conjured him up, there he was, standing in front of them.

"Oh, hi!" Moose exclaimed, just as startled as they were to run into each other, but then he smiled warmly at Georgia, his eyes crinkling up just a little in the corners as he took her in. "You're looking great. How are you?"

Georgia just stared at him. He was acting like nothing had happened; that everything was fine.

Her mind broke a little, trying to take that in.

And then…

"You'd know how I was if you'd ever called," she snapped.

"Or came by the credit union!" She wanted to scream and yell and beat him about the head with something heavy and most of all, she wanted to throw herself into his arms and hug him close...

Which just frustrated her even more.

I don't need him. I don't. I really don't.

And she was totally going to believe herself any minute now.

Any second...

CHAPTER 21

MOOSE

EVERY PLEASURE CENTER in Moose's brain had lit up like the 4th of July when he'd spotted Georgia. He'd been coming out of the corner store after picking up a gallon of milk and a loaf of bread for tomorrow's breakfast, while also doing his best to avoid all of the traffic from the wine tasting and art walk.

His landlord had warned him that it'd be starting Memorial weekend, and not to drive his truck anywhere after five because his parking spot would be gone as soon as he pulled out. Moose'd figured his landlord probably knew what he was talking about after years of living through these events, so he'd walked the three blocks down to the corner store to get some milk.

He'd spent the walking time worrying through everything he still needed to do before he could reach out to Georgia. Life had changed so drastically, it was a little hard to wrap his mind around the extent of his to-do list. He needed to get his oil changed on his truck, and do a full grocery run in the next couple of days, and then—

None of his internal mumblings and worry about what to do and when to do it seemed important, though, as soon as he'd seen Georgia. He wasn't supposed to be talking to her yet – he was trying to be a good boy and not talk to her until he'd earned it, dammit – but almost running over her in the crowd… he just couldn't walk away.

He was strong, but not *that* strong.

Instead of her face lighting up with the same pleasure and excitement he felt thrumming through him, though, Georgia seemed…distinctly pissed off.

What in the ever-living hell is going on here?

"I haven't had a chance to come by yet," he said slowly, confused about where the anger was coming from. "I've been busy moving."

"Moving? Are you and Tennessee getting married that quickly, then? Moving in together right away?" Her arms were folded across her chest and she was staring up at him, her eyes flashing with hurt and pain, and then Tripp muscled his way between them.

"Maybe you two should talk some other time," Tripp growled, his arms also folded across his chest. "That is, *if* Georgia wants to."

Moose's gaze skittered up and down the muscle-bound man in front of him, trying to decide if he could take him out with one punch or if it'd need two, when Georgia pulled him back out of the way. "Tripp, I appreciate it," she said, patting his arm, stoking the flames of jealousy ever higher in Moose – *I could break that arm into a million little*— "but I've got this." She turned back to Moose with a glare that did *not* bode well, and then she opened up her delectable mouth and ripped into him.

"You, Deere Garrett, I could just—"

"Rocky," he said baldly. He didn't know why he was interrupting her. He knew it was a shitty idea. A dumb, deaf, and blind man would know it was a shitty idea, but still, he couldn't help himself. Here he was, working his ass off for her, and she was acting like he was in the wrong.

Hell no, he wasn't about to take that sitting down.

"What?!" She stared at him, her mouth gaping open.

"Deere *Rocky* Garrett. If you're going to yell at me and use my proper name, I just figured you oughta get the whole thing in there."

Her mouth opened and closed a few more times, no sounds coming out, and then she *really* began to unload.

"Deere *Rocky* Garrett," she sneered, "you up and disappeared without a word. I told you to talk to Tenny and then call me, but next thing I know, here comes your father storming into my office, yelling his head off and trying to intimidate me, and where are you? Nowhere to be found. Not a phone call to be had! Not even a damn text!" She poked him in the chest. "You can't pull that kind of stunt, you asshole!"

"Hold on a minute!" Moose protested. "My father came down and talked to you?"

And then the green-eyed monster inside of him roared to life as he watched Tripp drape his arm around Georgia's shoulders, pulling her to his side protectively like he had every right to touch her.

Dammit all, Georgia had always claimed that they were "only friends," but tonight, Tripp was acting like any boyfriend would to protect his girl. The way Moose would be acting if the shoe were on the other foot.

He sneered at the man, his hands balling at his sides.

Pretty boy. All muscle, no skill. He spends all of his time lifting weights in the gym but I spent most of my childhood wrestling with Levi. I could beat this pretty boy with one arm tied behind my back. If he kisses her in front of me, I swear I'll kill him with my bare hands.

"Yes," Georgia said impatiently. "Right after you told him I *ordered* you to break up with Tennessee. Asshat! Need I remind you, I did not say that, nor would I."

"I didn't tell him that!" Moose exclaimed, reluctantly pulling his gaze away from the possessive grip Tripp had on Georgia's shoulders, and locking eyes with her instead. He had to concentrate. He had to figure out where this'd all gone wrong.

He could beat Tripp into a bloody pulp later. "Dammit, Georgia, listen to me. Why would I say that to my dad? You told me it was *important* to talk to Tennessee; you didn't *order* me to break up with her."

"So what, are you calling your father a liar?" Georgia demanded, one eyebrow raised as she stared up at him defiantly.

"Yes," he shot back. "Are you calling me a liar?"

She shifted from foot to foot, clearly debating what she should say in response to that. Tripp squeezed her shoulders, whispered into her ear, and Moose watched as she nodded, whispered back, and then Tripp disappeared into the crowd.

"Your date going home?" Moose asked sarcastically, the acid of the words burning a hole through his chest.

"At least he doesn't pull a disappearing act on me whenever his father scares him into submission," Georgia threw right back.

Shit. Why did Pretty Boy have to up and disappear like that? Moose wanted to plant his fist into someone's face, and Georgia's wouldn't exactly do.

He closed his eyes and drew in a deep breath, then let it out slowly, trying to force the anger boiling inside of him down; shove it into a corner. This wasn't like him, and a small part of his brain – the part not under siege from uncontrollable jealousy – understood that.

He'd never been jealous before, and he couldn't rightly say he was enjoying the feeling. Tennessee could've made out with some dude in front of him and he probably would've just let out a yawn.

But seeing Tripp put his arm around Georgia's shoulders?

Acid and rage.

He took another deep breath. Remembering Tripp's arm around Georgia's shoulders wasn't helping anything.

He had to focus. Something was wrong here. Even through the swirling currents of anger, Moose could tell that. He had to concentrate on what had gone wrong and fix it. *Then* he could go beat Pretty Boy into the ground.

He held up his loaf of bread and jug of milk, the cold of the milk jug handle making his hand ache. Why hadn't he thought to wear gloves? "I'd just grabbed a few groceries when I saw… you." He decided it was best for all involved to leave Tripp out of the discussion. "Will you walk with me?"

"To your truck?" she asked, confused.

"No, back home to my apartment," he said, impatient. "It's just up and over a couple of blocks."

"You moved to Franklin?"

He noticed she hadn't moved an inch.

"Of course. What did you think I'd been doing for the last two weeks?" he practically growled.

"I don't know – getting married to Tennessee! Starting your own John Deere Dealership! Moving to New York City to become a Broadway actor! How the hell am I supposed to know? You didn't call to tell me anything!"

Oh.

Oh.

Ohhhhhh…

Shit, Moose, you really are stupid some days.

His anger drained away as they locked eyes, just staring at each other on the streets of Franklin, every passerby an audience to it all.

"Do you love Tripp?" He blurted the words out, and in that moment, couldn't muster up the self-control to regret it.

He had to know.

"Moose, I'm honestly hard-pressed to say that I like *any* male on the planet at this moment."

He laughed a little at that. "Knowing the male species," he said dryly, "I rather think we deserve that."

But she didn't love Tripp. It was in her eyes. He was sure of it. He still wanted to punch the man once or twice – or a half-dozen times, honestly – but that was just for the crime of touching Georgia in front of him.

Whether Tripp was madly in love with his boss or not didn't matter. She didn't love him.

Moose could breathe again.

He reached up to stroke Georgia's cheek and ended up whacking her instead with the loaf of bread. "Sorry!" he yelped, yanking the bread back. They both froze for a minute, each trying to decide what to say and where their relationship was going and what the other person was thinking, and then Moose whispered, "Just walk with me."

It was almost begging – it *was* begging – but Georgia was worth losing a little of his pride over.

"It's just a few blocks over, I promise. Then I'll walk you back to your car. Or did Tripp drive you here?"

He worked hard to ignore the sharp stab of jealousy at the thought. *You've screwed this up too badly to be jealous. If she chose to move on, that's what you get for being a dumbass.*

It didn't mean he was enjoying this, though.

"He did drive us here," Georgia acknowledged, the iciness of her tone unmistakable, "but he's headed back to Sawyer already. I'll call a cab to drive me back when we're done talking."

Hell. Tripp really was giving them the space to talk without hanging on as a third wheel. Moose was grateful, if not more than a little confused. If Tripp was in love with Georgia, he sure had a funny way of showing it.

"Let's head to my place then," Moose said as Georgia hunted for an official return spot to put her empty wine glass. She finally spotted one, trotted over to put it down, and then rejoined him. Moose couldn't help following her every step with hungry eyes. She looked better than he'd remembered…

And he wouldn't have believed that could be possible.

They started down the street together, quickly leaving the

majority of the crowds behind, Moose's groceries swinging with each step.

"I'm not sure what my father told you," Moose said finally, after turning the situation over and over in his mind, trying to figure out how to best tackle this. He couldn't screw it up. There was something completely wrong here, and he had to be sure not to make things even worse with the slip of the tongue or one wrong statement. "Whatever it was that he said, I'm sure it wasn't complimentary. Let me tell you what really happened, and you decide from there."

He started the retelling with the evening that he'd talked to Tennessee, going home to angry parents afterwards, his father suddenly "wanting some time to think about it," and then the next day when he'd told Moose he'd inherit nothing.

He was dying a little inside as they wandered along in the deepening evening light – did she believe him? Was she just letting him ramble on to be polite, but would tell him which bridge to jump off when he was done?

He couldn't tell – the shadows on her face were too deep. She was a blank wall of nothingness.

"That day when he was going to 'think about things' must've been when he went over to talk to you. I...I was so stupid. I'd honestly thought he was trying to get used to the idea that his son would care about who he married. I had no idea he was trying to intimidate you into helping force Tennessee and me back together. I didn't know, I swear."

Still nothing.

He hurried on, desperate to fill the silence.

"I left that night and drove over to Levi's. I was...I was lost. I may've hated being under my father's thumb all this time, but honestly, it's a little scary outside of it, too. Georgia, I've never rented my own apartment, bought my own groceries, worried about my credit, tried to find a job...all of the things that come along with adulthood? I skipped it all. None of that was needed when I was working for Dad and living at home;

none of it was possible when I was working 18 hours a day, anyway.

"I had no idea what my next move should be. Was I going to go back to work at the dealership the next morning? Act like nothing had happened? My back was against the wall, and it was time to start making decisions."

He took a deep breath, letting it puff out in a cloud of moisture in the cold night air as they walked. His fingers were aching from gripping the cold handle of the milk jug, but he ignored the pain.

"Levi let me sleep on his couch, no questions asked. The next day, he went to work while I stayed behind, trying to decide what I was doing with my life. I'd thought that I was prepared to lose the dealership; I'd thought that I'd made my brain and soul realize that something I was working for my entire life might be gone in the blink of an eye. But until it really happened…"

He let out a deep sigh.

"When I'd first walked out the door, I was on this euphoric high – I'd stood up to my father! I'd walked away from him! It was a really great feeling…right up until the adrenaline drained out and I realized everything that I'd just lost. I had no idea how hard that would be. I guess a part of me just didn't believe my father would really do it."

The shock of it all, still reverberating through him two weeks later, made him clench his fist even tighter around the freezing cold handle of the milk jug. He'd probably have to peel his fingers off the jug one by one when they got to his apartment, but at the moment, he just didn't care.

How could he? How could my father have done this to me?

"I still can't figure out what his game plan is," he said aloud, not willing to voice the pain that his dad had caused. Anger was okay to show. Pain…it meant he was vulnerable. "Pride means everything to him. If me or Rhys don't take the dealership over, it means admitting to the world that his sons

want nothing to do with him. After all, it is the *Garrett* Tractor &
Implement Dealership. That's my father to a T – so arrogant, he
slapped our last name on the side of the building. He knows
that if someone from outside of the family bought it they'd
change the name. Deep down, I never believed his pride would
allow that."

They'd finally arrived at the old house that'd been long ago
chopped up into apartments, a set of creaky wooden stairs
leading up to the main floor while a staircase wound its way
down to the basement underneath them.

He paused at the base of the stairs, suddenly embarrassed.
This was not a palatial home. Not like his parents'. He—

Georgia put her hand on his arm and spoke, the first words
she'd said since he'd started talking. "I'm happy to see your
new apartment," she said softly. "It's an apartment earned with
your two hands. I'm proud of you."

He nodded politely, but didn't believe a word of it. Sure, it
was sweet of her to say that, but she hadn't been inside yet.

Biting back his reluctance, he led the way up the rickety old
stairs. Shit, what if his dad ever saw where he lived? He'd hit
the roof, apoplectic that his own son'd stained the family honor
by living in the slums.

And his mother…well, she wouldn't say her judgmental
thoughts out loud, but they'd be there in her eyes.

He definitely couldn't bring his parents here. Not ever.

He shoved his key into the lock and with a deep breath,
opened the door, following her inside with his minimal
groceries in hand. It was a simple layout – a living room and
kitchen combo upfront, with a short hallway leading to the
bathroom and bedroom in the back. It was a step up from a
studio apartment, but not much of one.

Georgia looked around as he shoved the milk in the fridge
and tossed the bread on the counter, flexing his hand to bring
the circulation back as he watched her take in the worn couch
and wooden crate serving as his coffee table, not even a TV on

the wall. He'd been picking up pieces from the thrift store as he could, practically haunting its aisles, trying to find furniture that wasn't ripped from the 70s to decorate with.

"It's not much—" he began defensively, and she looked back at him, a huge smile on her face.

"But it's yours, at least for now. Moose, I am so damn proud of you."

"You—you are?" he repeated, dumbfounded. "But there's a crack in the wall, and the mattress in the bedroom is still on the floor because I haven't bought a bed frame yet, and—"

Georgia stepped in front of him and placed a finger on his lips, immediately damming the flow of words. He wanted to flick his tongue out and suck her finger into his mouth, but he wouldn't let himself do it.

He hadn't earned that right. Yet.

"You and your father are more alike than I think you realize," she said softly.

"What?!" Thems were fightin' words, and he felt his blood pressure skyrocket at the mere suggestion. "I am *not*—"

"No, you are not Rocky Garrett," she cut in. "But in too many ways, you think like him. Moose, I don't care how big or grand your house is. I care who you are. You are the man who stood up to his overbearing father. You are the man who saved me from a wildfire. You are the man who gave up his inheritance for me. Yeah, maybe you haven't explained yet why it is that you pulled a disappearing act on me for the past two weeks—"

"I-was-trying-to—"

She pushed her finger harder to his lips, and he shut up.

"But before you grovel and tell me why you were such a dipshit for the past two weeks, we're going to get something out of the way."

Since she didn't seem too keen on letting him speak, he raised his eyebrows in question instead.

"You're going to kiss me, and we're going to decide if all of this was worth it. We're here on a wing and a prayer, and maybe—"

Which was when Moose decided that it was Georgia's turn to shut up.

He swung her up into his arms, grinning at her yelp of surprise, and carried her the few steps to the piece-of-shit couch that also happened to be comfy as hell. He sank down into it with her in his arms, pulling her gently to him and settling his lips over hers.

He didn't know what he expected when he kissed Georgia Rowland, but…this was not it.

He never could've expected this.

CHAPTER 22
GEORGIA

MOOSE PULLED HER DOWN onto his lap and settled her against him, his dick quickly gaining an interest in the proceedings under her ass as he dipped his head down, his lips grazing softly over hers.

She didn't know what to expect when he kissed her – excitement? Pleasure? Happiness? – but whatever she had expected, it was all of that...and so much more. After a painful decade of watching him and her cousin together at every event and knowing that he could never be hers, that she was a terrible human being for even wanting him to be hers...

This kiss was all that she'd wanted, but all the better because it was *real*. It was more vibrant, more vivid, more overwhelming than any daydream she'd ever indulged in.

She was home.

She was his.

She was never going to leave.

"Georgie," he breathed, his mouth warm against her skin as he trailed a path of kisses down her neck, and she decided instantly that the nickname that she'd always hated was actually quite lovely indeed. "I need to tell you..."

He stopped kissing her, his forehead resting against her

neck, his breath hot and fast, and she wanted to cry or scream or beat her fists against his chest for stopping, but she didn't. She held still, waiting for him to spill the beans so they could get on with it.

Preferably before she shook to pieces with need.

"I've-only-done-this-once."

The words came out in a rush, almost unintelligible. She forced her lust-addled brain to think through what he'd said, and then assign meaning to his words.

"You've…you've only had sex once?" she finally got out. That couldn't be right, of course. He and Tenny had dated for years. A decade. You didn't make it through your horny teenage years with a steady girlfriend, and only have sex once. Hell, her and Levi had gone at it like rabbits more times than she could ever hope to count, and they hadn't been a couple for nearly as long as Moose and Tennessee had.

His forehead brushed against her neck as he nodded, though, and she sucked in a quick breath at the movement. *But, that can't be…it couldn't…*

"Did you guys make some sort of vow or something?" Suddenly, it felt awkward to be on his lap while having this kind of discussion. She scooted off his lap, heaving a mental sigh at what she was leaving behind. It'd been a damn long while since she'd had any attention beyond the battery-powered kind.

This close…

"Not a vow, exactly." He was staring straight ahead, not turning to look her in the eye, and the tips of his ears were tinged pink.

The sexiest guy in high school is blushing while talking about sex.

I can't ever tell anyone about this conversation; not only because I can't share something this personal, but no one would believe me anyway.

After it became clear that this was as far as Moose was going to get on his own, Georgia spoke again.

"If not a vow, then what?" She worked hard to modulate her voice and not show the frustration building inside of her. She'd been *so close* to finally breaking the world's longest dry spell – or so it'd felt like to her, although she was starting to learn that somehow, some way, the sexiest fireman in Long Valley had gone through a longer one.

"We weren't...compatible."

"I know." Now the frustration *was* bleeding through, but she couldn't make herself care. Now was *not* the time to be discussing Moose and Tenny's failed relationship. They'd been on the road to some hot-and-heavy bedroom action, dammit, and to sit around and discuss why these two hadn't worked out was not exactly top-of-list for Georgia. "That's why you two finally got up the courage to break things off. You weren't compatible as a couple."

"No." He shook his head. "Well, yes. That too. But I mean...I didn't fit. Inside of her. When we tried, I didn't fit, and she cried. A lot. We never tried again." His ears were now a brilliant red.

Oh.

Oohhhhhh...

Georgia blinked a couple of times, processing what he was telling her.

"She...she didn't tell me that," Georgia whispered. "The night at the fundraiser. Or ever, honestly. I always figured... Anyway, that's not the point," she said, waving away the rabbit trail that was her overly private cousin. Sometimes, Georgia wondered if she knew Tennessee at all. "This doesn't mean there's a damn thing wrong with you. Or with her. It's more common than you'd think, actually. Your shape, her shape, your size, her size...and the first time can be painful anyway, no matter what. Mine wasn't – I think I broke my hymen a long time ago considering how athletic I am."

"Hymen?" he repeated the clinical phrase quizzically, and finally turned to look at her.

"My cherry?" she clarified with a saucy wink. "I probably popped my cherry with all of the horseback riding that I did while I was in school. It happens a lot to girls." She shrugged. "Anyway, sex doesn't hurt me. That's the bottom line. That's what you're worried about, right? That there's something wrong with you?"

He nodded slowly. "Tenny wasn't interested in trying again, and I couldn't cheat on her, so…I helped myself along. A lot." He flashed her a rueful grin. "I was still a horny teenage boy. That didn't change."

Georgia reached up and stroked his cheek. "A lot of guys would've pushed her anyway," she said softly. "It means a lot that you didn't."

"Don't paint me as too much of a saint," he said with a warning chuckle. "I wanted to. God, it was hard. Figuratively and literally." He winked, and then his grin faded away. "I worried constantly about what would happen. After we got married, I mean. Would I end up in a loveless marriage? What if she *never* enjoyed it? I couldn't rape my own wife." He shuddered, his voice thick with emotion. "We were so damn wrong together. On every level."

Georgia smiled slightly as she ran her fingertips over his lips. "You were," she agreed baldly. "But tonight, you'll find that there isn't a damn thing wrong with you. I promise, I won't be crying by the end of this."

"Good," he whispered, and then closed his eyes and sucked in a breath, the relief visibly washing over him. "Good," he whispered again, and this time, when he opened his eyes, they were hot with need.

"Good is right," Georgia whispered back. "Now, get over here and kiss me like you mean it."

He leaned over and easily plucked her off the couch and settled her back onto his lap, laughing at her gasp of surprise. "*That* is something I can get behind," he said, winking.

His lips skimmed over hers but before she could open up

and let him come inside, he instead drifted across her cheek and then down her neck, sucking and nibbling and blowing lightly as his mouth left a trail of heat and desire across her skin. With a groan, she tilted her head, giving him better access, and then he was skimming his lips across her collarbone. "You," he breathed, "are so damn beautiful. Do you know how long I've wanted to do this?"

His lips were drifting lower and he was tugging her shirt out of the way, trying to reach her skin as she lit up inside, as every pleasure center in her brain went haywire, overloaded by the sheer joy and lust and desire pulsating through her. She pulled him closer to her, wanting to crawl inside of him somehow; become one with him. Being separated from him, even just by clothes, suddenly seemed like the biggest tragedy she'd ever lived through.

She pulled away and began tearing frantically at his clothes and at hers, hearing a rip and not knowing where it came from and definitely not caring. All that mattered was being able to feel his skin against hers...

Finally, she managed to get his shirt off him and began running her fingers up his skin, the muscles jumping under her fingertips. "Ohhh..." he groaned, his eyes fluttering shut. He leaned his head against the back of the couch, letting her feel her way over his body. "I've wanted this...my whole life, I think."

The softness of his skin overlying the bulk of his muscle, and a bit of hair on top of it all...it was heaven to explore. She leaned forward and pressed her lips against his chest and he let out a groan that vibrated through his whole body and up through her lips, muscles tensing beneath her. She opened her eyes just a bit and peered down, noticing that his hands were clenched into fists at his sides, and she grinned to herself. To see a man like Moose desire her this much...

No, she'd never expected anything like this at all.

She moved her lips over to his flat nipples, one and then the other, suckling on them, running her tongue over their rigid tips as his dick grew just as rigid under her ass and his breathing grew shallow and his fists curled into tighter balls.

"Oh…Georgie…oh…Georgie…" he panted, his eyes screwed shut, and she decided that she liked that nickname more than anything else in the world. "I didn't know…if I'd known…I never would've waited so long…please…" His breaths were short, his chest rising and falling with each gasp and she grinned to herself as she moved lower down his body. She slid off the couch and landed on her knees in front of him, and then began pulling at the buckle and zipper of his Wranglers.

"Yes…no…please…" he begged and she let out a little laugh. She, the ugly cousin, had done this to Moose.

Yeah, she was feeling pretty damn good about herself.

Between the two of them, they wiggled his jeans and boxer-briefs down to his ankles where they were caught up by his boots and then she was staring in appreciation at his dick. A little precum was hanging off the tip while the rosy red length was pulsating with every beat of his heart, practically straining towards her.

"Am I too—" he started, but she interrupted him. Not with words – she was past words – but with her mouth. As she wrapped her mouth around his rock-hard dick, he jerked off the couch, hips bucking as he groaned loudly with pleasure.

He wasn't speaking anymore, and neither was she. Words were too difficult. Too complicated. All that was left was desire.

Well, and a little bit of fear. As she worked her mouth and throat and hands up and down his length, she knew why Tenny had such problems with his size. He was bigger than Levi – thicker. Longer. Bigger than any guy Georgia had ever seen. Maybe…

Maybe he wouldn't fit after all.

And then his hips were jerking and spasming beneath her as he shouted, arching, his cum shooting down her throat as she held onto his hips, keeping her mouth on him through it all.

Finally, he went slack and dropped back against the couch, a grin of such self-satisfied delight on his face that Georgia couldn't help but laugh.

"I'm sorry," he mumbled, his eyes still closed. "I know a lady always goes first. I just..." He sighed, and she laughed again.

He peered at her through the sliver of one eyeball. "After all this time, you have no idea..."

"Did Tennessee not like giving head either?"

She hadn't meant to ask. The question just popped out. She didn't want to know, anyway. She didn't want to know anything more about her cousin's sex life.

But, she also couldn't *quite* make herself open her mouth and take back her question. Funny, that.

He shook his head woefully. "A little hand job every once in a while, but usually, that was reserved for my birthday. She never enjoyed it, though. She tried to pretend enthusiasm, but this was the one time where I could see right through her. Nothing in the world is sexier than someone desiring *you*. She never did."

Sitting back on her heels, Georgia could only shake her head in disbelief. Her cousin was an idiot; there were no two ways about it. Her gaze drank in his body – the dips and ridges and valleys everywhere, just begging to be explored with her tongue and her fingers and her eyes and he was hers, all hers – and then his dick began to harden again under her gaze. Her eyes shot to his and he sent her a leering grin that made her laugh. "I've been wanting this for a damn long time," he said, and then bent over and ripped at his shoelaces on his boots. "I'm nowhere close to being done with you." He toed off his boots, pulled his jeans off and tossed them into the corner, and then he was scooping her up into his arms for a second time that evening, this time to carry her to the bedroom.

"I can walk, you know," she told him primly, even as she grinned to herself with pleasure. The feminist inside of her would never admit it out loud, of course, but she loved being carried around by him.

"What would the fun in that be?" he asked when they'd covered the few steps into the bedroom and he could begin stripping what was left of her clothing off her. "When you're walking, I can't snuggle you against my chest; I can't feel your curves or your skin; I can't move you wherever I want. That takes all the fun out of it."

She laughed and then said mock-seriously, "I can see why you would feel that way. It's important to take all of that into consideration…"

He pulled her panties off – a little piece of lace nothin' that she rarely wore but had picked out for tonight's outing over her normal granny panties, thank God – and then began crawling over the bed towards her, growling as he went. "I believe you have something I want," he said, his chest vibrating with the sounds as he hovered over her.

"Oh yeah?" she said, a squeak betraying her at the end. She cleared her throat and tried it again. "What's that?"

"Your pussy."

"Oh!" Her face flushed pink and he grinned lasciviously down at her.

"Your face matches your pussy when you get embarrassed," he told her.

Which was right about the time that her face flushed an even deeper red.

He laughed.

"If I hurt you," he murmured, sending puffs of warm air over her labia, "I want you to tell me. I couldn't stand to hurt you."

"Moose?" she panted.

"Yes?" He stopped nosing through her curls and looked up at her.

"If you don't stop talking, I'm going to kill you."

"Fair enough," he said with a laugh, and then began working his tongue up and down her, following the writhing of her hips as she screamed with joy.

He's all mine…all mine…all mine…

"Can't…wait…" he panted and crawled up over her, and she tensed for just a moment, the haze of lust dissipating as she worried about his size.

What if he *was* too big?

And then he was smoothly thrusting inside of her and he fit perfectly, stretching her and it felt oh so good, the kind of pleasure she hadn't felt in a long time. Maybe, a tiny part of her brain added, not ever. This felt better than it ever had with Levi, and she locked her legs around his hips and rode him, letting the joy of it all roll over her like a wave onto the shoreline. He strained, stopping, jerking inside of her, face a frozen mask of pure pleasure and no one was breathing, no one at all, until he finally relaxed and collapsed against her.

It was just the two of them, sweat sticking their skin together, as he rolled over and pulled her against his chest and they fell asleep, curled around each other, them against the world.

CHAPTER 23
MOOSE

H E DRIFTED SLOWLY to the surface on a haze of pleasure, trying to revel in it while also putting his finger on… something. Something that was wrong. It was niggling at him, taunting him from the sleepy corners of his brain, and if he could just reach out and grab it…

"Georgia!" he whispered urgently, shaking her shoulder. "Georgia, you gotta wake up."

"Huh?" she mumbled and rolled over to crack her eyes open up at him. "Whatswrong?" she sleep mumbled, even as the tiny crack in her eyelids fluttered closed again.

"I didn't use a condom!" he said urgently, trying to keep the panic under control. He shook her shoulder again. "I might've just made you pregnant!"

With a sigh of regret, Georgia pushed herself up into a sitting position. "What time is it?" she asked around a jaw-cracking yawn.

His eyes flicked over to the nightstand and then back to her. "It's 2:35." He wanted to shake her again. She obviously didn't understand the importance of what he was trying to tell her.

"You woke me up at 2:35 in the morning to tell me that you forgot to use a condom and you may've made me pregnant?"

She yawned again, and Moose wondered for a moment if he'd actually spotted her tonsils or not. He kinda thought that he had. "Don't you think I noticed that you didn't put on a rubber? You really weren't kidding when you said you didn't know much about girls."

"Hey, I didn't say that," he protested defensively. "I said that Tenny and I only had sex once. There's a difference."

"Doesn't appear to be much of one to me right now," she grumbled. "Moose, I'm not pregnant, I promise. I've been on the pill for a long time now. It helps regulate my cycle. Otherwise, I'm all over the place. Why—" She paused to yawn again. "Why did you think we needed to have this discussion at two in the morning?"

"Oh." Dead quiet for the space of two heartbeats as he tried to think of how to say it delicately. "I...uhhh...thought after what happened with Levi, that you being pregnant would be a really big thing and I just...didn't think so much as panic." He sent her an apologetic smile. "You can go back to sleep now, I promise."

Bringing up the hardest part about his decision to choose Georgia over Tennessee – losing out on a chance to have children of his own – wasn't exactly at the top of his to-do list at this time of the night (or ever, really) but he'd also finally won his chance at a happily-ever-after with Georgia. His lizard brain had considered that to be a Code Red, and the adrenaline had flushed through him.

Now that he was sure it wasn't going to be a problem, he felt embarrassment overtake the panic that had been welling up inside of him. He really had made a muck of things.

She shoved a hand through her hair and then rubbed her eyes with the backs of her hands. "Sorry, what thing with Levi?" she asked sleepily. She wasn't lying back down and closing her eyes, which he kinda wished she'd do, and just forget any of this had happened.

Luck was not on his side.

"You know, when you turned down Levi's marriage proposal."

Talking about his best friend's marriage proposal to Georgia while they were both naked and sweaty from making love to each other…it felt wrong on so very many levels. Maybe that'd be enough of an answer to Georgia's questions, though, and she'd go back to sleep now.

She sat up straighter in bed. "What? What about Levi's marriage proposal?" The sleepy-eyed look she'd been giving him disappeared and was replaced by total confusion.

He wasn't so sure that was an improvement.

"You know, when Levi proposed to you…?"

"Yeah, I'm pretty sure I was there for that. What the hell does that have to do with pregnancy?"

"You told him you didn't want children." Even as he was explaining the obvious to her, he made himself the solemn vow that in the future, no matter how important he thought a question was, he shouldn't ask Georgia about it in the middle of the night. She wasn't one to just let it go and fall back asleep.

In fact…

She was staring at him like he'd quit speaking English on her. "You…I…What?!" she finally yelped. "I told Levi that I didn't want to have kids?!"

"Maybe?" Based on her reaction, he was thinking that this long-held belief of his was about to get shot down in flames.

She started laughing, but it was a disbelieving laugh, not a this-is-so-funny laugh.

He *really* didn't take that as a good sign.

"Men are the strangest creatures," she muttered to herself as she swung her legs out of bed. "If I'm going to have this conversation at—" she looked at his nightstand clock for herself this time, "—2:51 in the morning, I'm damn well going to have some coffee in me. You've bought a coffee pot for your apartment, I'm assuming?" She pushed herself to her feet and started heading for the bedroom door.

"Of course," he said, hurrying after her. It was the first purchase he'd made. He could sleep on the floor. He couldn't live without coffee.

Priorities. They were a thing.

He felt weird walking around his house naked, his dick swinging all over the place, so he slipped back and grabbed a pair of basketball shorts and a sweatshirt and put them on before joining her in the kitchenette. She was hunting through the cupboards, looking for the coffee can, and he went to work next to her, helping her get the pot going.

"While we're waiting for that…" She turned and planted her hands on her gloriously naked hips and then glared at him. "Hold on, not fair," she said when she spied all of his clothes, and hurried back to the bedroom.

She emerged wearing only a button-up shirt of his which he usually reserved for more formal occasions, leaving her legs bare beneath the soft cotton. He gulped hard and his vision went a little fuzzy around the edges. He thought about sending her back into the bedroom to put on more clothing – preferably a snowsuit if she thought they were going to engage in a serious conversation – but couldn't quite make himself do it.

Yes, it was torture to see her in one of his shirts, bare legs stretching for a mile beneath it, but it was a glorious torture, and so very worth it.

He filled a coffee cup up for her and then jerry-rigged some sweetener by using the milk he'd bought hours before and some brown sugar he'd mistakenly bought from the grocery store. "Brown sugar?" she asked, arching an eyebrow. "Were you going to bake some cookies?"

He waved his hand dismissively. "I'll tell you about it later." By which he meant absolutely never, upon the pain of death. Going shopping for his own food at the grocery store – yet another thing he'd done for the first time ever in the last two weeks – well, suffice it to say that some mistakes were made.

Best to leave it at that.

He poured himself some coffee in his only other mug, feeling rather proud of himself for having two coffee mugs in his cupboards to use, and followed her to the couch. She curled up, tucking her bare legs underneath her as she sipped at the coffee. Moose did his best not to blow a brain circuit – or two – at the sight as he settled in beside her.

"I don't know what Levi told you about his proposal, but I'm going to guess that it wasn't the whole story," she started. "Either he didn't understand, or he's forgotten. Unlike your father, I don't think Levi would intentionally lie to you. No offense intended," she added quickly.

"None taken, promise." He knew better than anyone in the world how his father could twist the truth to serve his purposes. Trust his father, after Rocky'd spent his whole life lying to his oldest child?

Not damn likely.

She nodded and settled back a little more against the couch. "You know that Levi and I started dating at the end of our junior year. What you don't know is that…honestly, I don't know if I ever really loved him. We had a lot of fun together and he was great in bed – not that I'm gonna talk to *you* about that – but it was never quite right, and it got less right as time went on. He became…comfortable. One of my closest friends who I also happened to kiss." She shrugged. "Although I thought he was a terrific guy, I didn't think he was my forever guy, but there was nothing to drive me away – nothing to force my hand. We were just drifting along.

"So you know that when we went to college – TIG welding for him, Business Administration for me – we obviously ended up at different colleges, which meant that the drift factor went up even further. We weren't just drifting along – we were drifting apart." Moose listened, nodding and trying to hide the anxiety he felt at her mention of college. His father had said that college wasn't necessary for Moose to be able to take over the dealership, and so he'd been left behind in Sawyer as Tennessee,

Levi, and Georgia had all left to get their degrees. They'd all come back, thank God, but there was a part of him that still felt...inferior for not having a degree to claim as his.

"Well, Levi never told me this for sure, but my best guess is, with his mom running off when he was just a babe and his dad being...well, the town drunk, honestly, I think Levi wanted to establish a family for himself. Something that couldn't be taken away from him. Something that didn't involve his father."

She chuckled without humor. "I know your dad isn't exactly stellar father material, but I'll say it again: I am very glad that he took Levi under his wing and paid for his training like he did. If it'd been up to that pile-of-shit father that he somehow won at birth, Levi'd still be at home, probably bagging groceries and spending all of his money keeping his father supplied with alcohol. Maybe even on the way to becoming an alcoholic himself."

She took a sip of her coffee and paused, thoughts skittering past on her face, too fast to capture and examine. He found watching her absolutely fascinating, and regretted even blinking, because it meant missing something.

"You know how Levi is," she finally continued. "So... intense. He wasn't content to just drift along, and when he felt our relationship begin to really fall apart, he decided to propose to me. I think he thought that it'd bring us back together. A last-ditch attempt to save our relationship, you know? I told him no, of course, because I *couldn't* marry him. Not..."

The room was silent. *Heartbeat...heartbeat...*

"Not when I was in love with his best friend." She whispered it as she looked over at him and he froze, the coffee cup almost to his mouth but not quite there and he couldn't breathe or move or think.

She rushed on before he could make his body and brain do something useful again, like work.

"When he proposed, he said it in a funny way. Not, 'Will you marry me?' like a normal proposal but 'Will you be my wife and the mother of my children?' I'm sure he thought he was being sweet and if it'd been right between us, it would've been sweet.

"But I was all of nineteen years old, and the guy I'd drifted along with for years was pushing me to have his children. The guy that I didn't really even love, not like you should love the person you marry. It freaked me out, I'm not gonna lie. I blurted out the first thing that came to mind: I didn't want to have kids. So, in retrospect, I can see why he thought, well, that I didn't want to have kids."

She let out a small chuckle. "My brain wasn't operating at full speed at that point, but what I meant was, I didn't want to have kids when I was 19 years old, and I didn't want to have kids with him. I didn't mean that I didn't want to have children at all."

She nibbled at her lower lip as she thought through it. "In his defense, I didn't actually say that, now that I think back on it. It was the last conversation that we had for a very long time, and I'd honestly forgotten all about the specifics until just now." She shrugged, causing the open collar of his shirt to slide down her bare arm.

Moose gulped, trying to stay focused on what she was saying, and probably not succeeding as well as he should. He wanted to nibble his way up her arm and—

She continued, jerking his attention back to her story. "I knew what I meant, and calling him up to clarify, 'Hey Levi, when I said I didn't want to have kids, I really meant I didn't want them so soon or with you, so…have a great day!' Well, it didn't seem like the nicest thing in the world to do. Not to mention that at the heart of it, it really didn't matter. I didn't think about what he'd tell you, and even if I had, I still wouldn't have worried about it. After all, you were marrying Tenny."

She shrugged again, one tantalizing shoulder lifting with the movement before disappearing under the cover of fabric.

It was quiet for a minute then, as Moose tried to wrap his

mind around everything she'd just told him. She *did* want to have kids.

And, she'd loved him for years.

He wasn't sure which one of those statements thrilled him more.

"Do you…do you want to have children?" she asked hesitantly. "Just…someday. In the future. With someone. Hypothetically."

"Yeah, I really do," he said with a soft smile. "It was the one part about marrying Tennessee that I was excited about. I may not have thought she was the most beautiful woman in the world and the idea of having sex with her left me cold, but I was happy at the thought of being a father myself. I could do it right. I could treat my kids with respect and love, not as lowly paid servants. I want to teach them to work hard and be good citizens of the world, but I think you can do that without the belt and liberal doses of guilt and screaming. I wanted to see if I was right."

"You…you broke up with Tennessee, not only losing your parents and the dealership, but also believing that with me, you were going to give up the chance to have children, and yet, you still chose me?"

She was staring at him, surprise and shock openly battling for supremacy on her face. Then…

"Why?" she whispered, the disbelief obvious in every ounce of her being.

"Because I've always been in love with my best friend's girlfriend," he said simply. She sucked in a breath at that. He shrugged, offering up only a pained smile in response. "It didn't matter because I wasn't going to be able to choose who I married, and you and him were happy together, and…I just didn't have a chance. I thought all this time you'd been madly in love with him, and you only broke things off because of the kids' aspect. I thought you really, really cared about it, enough to break up with the man you desperately loved because of it."

"Wow." They stared at each other for a minute, and then a small smile grew into a huge grin which broke out into a howl of laughter. "By the very skin of our teeth," Georgia finally said as their stunned laughter died down. "If I hadn't been trapped by that fire and stuck out there with you overnight..."

He reached over and pulled her against his chest, spreading his legs out on the couch and tucking her slim body between them. "Sitting up at Eagle's Nest with you by my side was...it broke me. For years, I'd been able to ignore the desire I felt every time I looked at you and could convince myself I had to do my duty. But that night up on the mountain broke through that and no matter what I told myself afterwards, I couldn't stop myself from wanting you. I never thought I'd be grateful for a wildfire."

She laughed weakly against him. "Me either," she said softly. "I had flashbacks and panic attacks after the fire, and I thought for a while there that I'd never get over it. But I didn't guess that my life would change for the better because of it."

She put her coffee cup down on the weathered crate and nestled her head into the crook of his neck with a happy sigh. "I want to hear how you ended up here in Franklin," she mumbled. "Last I knew, your father was yelling at me that you'd never pick the ugly cousin and that he'd cut you off without a penny if you chose me. And then you disappeared."

He grimaced, glad she wasn't facing him to see the embarrassment on his face. "Maybe you're right, about being like my dad." He almost choked on the words, but damn his pride. It was how he'd gotten into this situation to begin with. "I was raised that you take care of the women in your household, and that they absolutely do not work outside of the home. I don't have anything against your career, of course, but I guess a part of that old-fashioned notion still clung to me. I didn't want to go to you and ask you to date me if I didn't even have a place to sleep at night that wasn't Levi's lumpy couch," she chuckled softly at that, "or a job to go to every day."

He began running his fingers through her hair, softly stroking down the blonde strands as he talked. "The day that Levi went to work and left me on his couch, I had a lot of thinking to do. A part of me knew that I could go back to Dad, apologize, swallow crow, and still inherit the dealership. Marrying Tennessee…I don't know if that would've ended up being a part of it or not. It would depend on her parents, and of course, Tennessee doesn't want to marry me any more than I want to marry her.

"But either way, I couldn't do it. I knew it was time to actually get out on my own. Make my own mistakes. And, like I said, I needed to find a place of my own that wasn't Levi's couch. At first, I couldn't think of what marketable skills I had."

He paused, the worry he'd felt that day as he mentally reviewed his choices overwhelming him again. A part of him had wondered if his father had pushed him not to get a college degree, knowing that it'd make it harder for Moose to strike out on his own if he ever decided to.

He wouldn't put it past his father, that was for damn sure. Manipulative to the bitter end.

He took a deep breath and continued. "I've worked in a lot of different departments at the dealership, but I wasn't a licensed anything. I'd have to go to school to become a licensed diesel mechanic; my father owned the only John Deere dealership in the area and I don't know a damn thing about any other kind of tractor; I didn't want to move to Boise and lose my chance with you…I spent the whole day spinning my wheels."

She snuggled against him, sighing happily, and he wondered for a moment if his story was putting her to sleep. He couldn't see her face very well from this angle. He kept talking and stroking her hair, though, because it was nice to talk to someone. He'd gotten lonely, living by himself.

If she drooled on him, though, he'd take that as a sign to carry her to bed. And anyway, picking her up in his arms and snuggling her against him as he walked was a nice consolation prize for having to stop talking to her for the night.

"It was Levi's suggestion, when he got home that evening. We've...not been seeing eye to eye recently," Moose said, choosing his words carefully, "and I was a little worried that the whole couch-crashing thing wouldn't go over well, but he didn't utter a single word of complaint about any of it. When he got home after work, I told him what happened – at least the most important parts – and then we began brainstorming on what jobs I could apply for.

"Like I said, it was his idea: I could go to work at the Massey Ferguson dealership here in Franklin. Yeah, maybe it's not John Deere, but they *are* tractors and when you get right down to it, the basics are the same. I applied for a salesman job and once the owner realized who my dad was, he hired me on the spot. Apparently, and I know this is going to be hard to believe, but my father is a jackass to the other tractor dealers in the area," she chuckled quietly at that, tucked up against his chest, "and the idea of giving my father the middle finger *really* appealed to the owner of the Massey dealership."

He didn't tell her about the heart-to-heart that he'd had with Levi about her. He wasn't sure if Georgia knew that Levi had been carrying a torch for her all of these years, but it wasn't Moose's place to tell her that. Let Levi keep his pride intact.

It hadn't exactly been a pleasant conversation, and a few punches had been thrown in the middle of it, but in the end, they'd worked things out. You couldn't be as close as brothers for 17 years, and then let a little thing like unrequited love get in the way.

"In fact," Moose continued, "the Massey owner even gave me an advance to help me pay the deposit on this apartment and put a little food in the fridge. I didn't have much in the way of savings, and this whole thing has blown a hole the size of Texas in my wallet. I gotta tell you the truth, Georgia: I don't have two nickels to rub together after my 'shopping spree' that

I did a couple of hours ago. I get my first real paycheck tomorrow, and never have I been more thrilled in my life. I'm finally making decent money. No more minimum wage for me."

He was running his calloused fingers through her wispy hair, the roughness catching on the strands and then slipping free. It was hypnotizing. Being with her brought him the kind of peace and joy he'd been wanting all his life, but had never been able to find.

"I cannot believe your father was paying you minimum wage. I knew he was a bastard, but that takes the cake. But," she waved a hand dismissively through the air, "that doesn't answer the question of why you didn't tell me what was going on." She yawned and then settled back against him. "You make a really nice pillow, by the way," she added sleepily.

"Maybe I'll add that to my resumé," he said with a small chuckle. "As for talking to you…well, I was going to. Right after I'd officially established myself here. I know it sounds stupid and in retrospect, it is, but I had it in my head that in order to date someone as successful and amazing as you, I needed my own place and a steady job and a pile of money in the bank account, and *then* I could come a-courtin'."

"'A-courtin'?" she repeated softly, laughing, jiggling against his chest in some very delightful ways. "You are adorably old-fashioned." She sat up, stretching, his shirt molding to her chest in an even more delightful way, and then she smacked him across the head.

"Oww!" he hollered in shock, rubbing his head. "What was that for?"

She settled back against his chest again. "For being an adorably old-fashioned idiot," she informed him. "You seemed to think I would know what was going on. Since you didn't deign to tell me, did you think someone else would?"

He shrugged. "It's Sawyer. I figured you knew as soon as I walked out of my parents' front door, like some sort of bat signal that lit up the sky. Rumors get around so quickly in Long Valley, I just thought you knew."

She reached up without even moving much this time, and lightly tapped him upside the head. "That's for being an adorably old-fashioned self-centered idiot," she said, snuggling back down against him. "People don't just stand around in the streets of Sawyer, ready to do nothing but spread the word about what's happening in Moose Garrett's life."

He scrunched up his nose at her words. She was right…even if it'd felt like that was *exactly* what happened when he was a teenager. He'd once gotten in trouble for agreeing to go to a drinking party being held one weekend on the beach of Sawyer Lake. He hadn't even gone but the news that he was planning to still made it back to his dad, and he'd been grounded for three weeks after having done absolutely nothing.

Thinking that the gossip chain kept tabs on him wasn't the fevered imagination of a self-centered idiot, but he took her reprimand for what it was – he should've told her what he was doing himself. Just one more mistake on the road to becoming a true adult; a road that seemed littered with hidden potholes and traps for the unsuspecting to fall into.

"So…you thought I was busy marrying Tennessee for the last two weeks?" he asked, and then laughed at the thought. "Sorry, I shouldn't laugh," he said quickly when she began to bristle up. "I just…I almost killed myself to get out of that relationship. The idea of marrying her is laughable to me at this point – literally."

"I knew you didn't want to, but the dealership and the approval of your father is a hell of an incentive to agree anyway. It would've been hard to say no to it," she pointed out logically.

"I didn't say no to it for the first 26 years of my life," he admitted. "Not something I'm proud of, but yeah, it's true."

They sat there in silence for a minute, until she slowly turned in his arms and looked up at him. "It may've taken you a while to get there, but at least you did eventually," she whispered, her eyes full of trust and love and admiration. He felt ten feet tall. "Plus, you saved Tenny from a marriage she did not want. She's probably more grateful to you than you could possibly know."

"Oh, I didn't even tell you – Tennessee compared me to a coffee table!" he said with a laugh. "That didn't exactly do wonders for my pride."

"A coffee table?" Georgia repeated with an incredulous smile. "You're definitely going to have to tell me the story behind that." But even as she was saying the words, she was leaning forward, running her fingertips up his chest and chasing them with her lips and Moose forgot how to breathe, and completely forgot what they were talking about. It was something…

Nope. Totally gone. All of his blood had officially gone south, leaving none for his brain. She wiggled up against him with a naughty smile. "I can tell you're thinking what I'm thinking."

"That this couch is way too small for the activity I have in mind?"

"Yeah, something like that," she breathed.

Just minutes later, as she was folded over the arm of the couch, her delicious ass in the air as he pounded into her from behind, all of the lust and desire that'd been suppressed for so long finally allowed to bubble up to the surface, he found out that the couch was just right…in other ways.

CHAPTER 24

MOOSE

"OKAY, YOU GUYS, let's talk about the best way to pull a hose from a truck," Jaxson said, standing near the rolled-up hose on the side of the main fire truck. "As you guys know, laying hose is backbreaking work *and* extremely important, which isn't always a great combo because the temptation is strong to—"

"Where is my dog?" a man demanded, bursting through the man door of the station. Everyone froze and then turned to him as one.

"Shiitttt," Moose heard Abby mutter to herself. He glanced over at her and she caught his eye. "Bad news," she mouthed.

The Long Valley County Deputy wasn't officially on the Sawyer firefighter crew, but often cross-trained with them to keep up on her EMT and first-aid certifications. Wyatt and their soon-to-be adopted son Juan were there that night with her, with both of them claiming to be thinking about joining the department.

Moose guessed that Wyatt just didn't want to be without his wife, and Juan didn't want to be without his parents, but hey, it was always fun to have more people at trainings, not less. Plus, with Jaxson reaching out to the younger kids in the area, like

Angus and Chris, bringing them onboard as junior firefighters, the idea of Juan joining the team wasn't really that far-fetched. He was just a kid, but starting 'em out young was never a bad idea.

All in all, it'd been a great training session…that is, until this drunk, one-tooth local yokel showed up.

"Is there something I can do for you?" Jaxson asked, stepping forward. Moose moved in beside him. As the deputy fire chief, he figured his place was next to the chief.

"I saw my dog in the newspaper," the man said, hitching up his belt and puffing up his chest. "Her picture and everythin' was in there. Y'all found her up in the hills, and I'm here to take her back."

Moose willed himself not to look towards the corner where Sparky had been curled up, sleeping with her head on Juan's lap, sharing the space with Maggie Mae, Wyatt's dog. They were tucked back far enough that they might be able to avoid detection from ol' eagle eyes here.

At the sound of the man's voice, though, Sparky let out a whimper and her tail started thumping against the concrete floor as she attempted to crawl up behind Juan and hide from her former owner. Maggie Mae, meanwhile, jumped to her feet in front of Juan and let out a low growl, her eyes watching the new arrival intently.

The man's eyes searched Sparky out in the darkened corner of the bay. "That was her just now!" he said triumphantly. "Always whining up a storm about somethin'. Worthless piece of shit." He started to walk towards Juan and the two dogs when Jaxson, Moose, and Troy moved as one to stand in his way.

"That article ran in the paper a month ago," Jaxson pointed out politely, keeping his voice calm. Even as Moose admired Jaxson's restraint, he was eyeing the douchebag in front of him, trying to decide if he should knee him in the nuts or the face. Hell, maybe he'd do both. After the bruises and damage Sparky had suffered, he rather figured the man deserved it. "Why so late in responding to it?"

"I don't take the paper," the man said with an insolent shrug. "I only seen it when my neighbor was rolling it out to use as a training pad for his new pup. That reporter sure made y'all sound like heroes," he added derisively, "especially Troy. Is that you?" He glanced up and down Jaxson, sizing him up. Moose's hands curled into fists at his sides.

"Nope, I'm Chief Jaxson Anderson. Troy is a firefighter on my crew, and he has adopted the dog in question. Now go on home and let's call it a night."

"I ain't just walkin' outta here without my huntin' dog," the man snarled. "She's mine. Had her since she was a pup."

"Did you make her scared of people?" Troy growled, and Moose almost swallowed his tongue. That was a complete sentence, with a beginning, a middle, and an end. He didn't realize the man knew how to string that many words together. "Sparky hates most men. Are you why?"

The man shrugged and hitched up his pants again. "I taught her a lesson or two," he allowed, "but only when she needed to learn 'em. That ain't the point. That's my dog, and I want her—"

"A hunting dog?" Abby asked, coming up on the other side of Troy. They'd formed a wall of muscle between the piece of shit and her adopted son and dogs. Moose grinned a little to himself. *Fight fair if you can, but cheat if you must,* drifted through his mind. He didn't feel too bad about cheating, honestly. It'd never been a fair fight between this man and Sparky, so why did he deserve a fair fight between him and the Sawyer firefighter crew?

Turnabout's fair play and all that karma shit.

"The day you lost her out in the foothills, were you out hunting?" Abby continued.

The man's eyes darted between them, clearly knowing where she was going with this and not quite sure how to get out of it. There were only a few animals on the Idaho Fish & Game's approved list that could be hunted so early in the year. Most hunters didn't hit the hills until fall when the deer and elk season opened up. The chances were roughly 100% or so that if he was hunting in May, he was hunting illegally.

"I...I were out target shootin'," he finally got out. He nodded, pleased as punch that he'd come up with a legal reason to be out shooting. "Cans and shit. Just workin' on my aim, was all."

"Did you happen to be off-roading while you were out target shooting?" Abby asked with a cocked eyebrow. "Did you happen to see your tailpipe setting fire to the dead grass as you went along?"

His face went white with shock as he realized that he'd dodged the hunting trap only to walk straight into the "Cause of a wildfire" trap.

"Hold on here a minute," he said, hitching his pants up so high, he was probably gonna be singing in the next octave up any moment now, "why am I talkin' to *you*? You ain't the police. What do you care where I drove my truck?"

She'd come to their training meeting tonight in civilian clothing since she wasn't currently on duty, which was probably the cause of the man's...lack of understanding and respect for who he was talking to.

Moose grinned with anticipation to himself. Abby wasn't someone to be trifled with, something this guy was about to figure out.

"I'm not a city cop, no," she said calmly, "but I *am* a county deputy. I'm surprised you don't remember me, Billy. After that last time when I got called out to your place 'cause you smashed in your neighbor's mailbox, I thought we'd become old friends."

Billy's face went even whiter as recognition sank in. "I knew I knew you from somewhere..." he grumbled under his breath.

His gaze skipped along the wall of muscle in front of him, clearly trying to decide what to do.

Abby must've thought it kind to help him along with the decision process, because she said blandly, "Did you know that if you off-road and your tailpipe starts a wildfire, that you're responsible for all of the costs of that fire? All of the men who worked to put it out, diesel for the vehicles, wear and tear… you're on the hook for it all. Are you *sure* you want to claim this dog, and implicate yourself as the cause of that fire? I think the county attorney could draw up a list of fees that you owe, if so.

"After all, this dog was found right next door to where the wildfire started, one where *three* agencies were called in to fight it. If it's your dog, then it's a pretty safe bet to say that it was also your tailpipe. Wouldn't you agree, Chief Anderson?" she asked, turning to Jaxson, making sure to put an extra emphasis on the title "Chief."

Before Jaxson could respond, the asshat began stumbling backwards in his haste to beat cheeks for the exit. "Damn dog were gun shy anyway," he tossed over his shoulder. "Good for nothin' piece of shit. You're welcome to her!" The man door banged closed behind him.

It was quiet for just a moment, and then everyone broke out laughing, the kind of laughter that hits after the awful stress of a situation disappears. Moose realized he could take a deep breath again, the fight-or-flight response slowly draining away.

"It's really too bad you can't actually go after Billy for that fire, and for animal abuse," Levi said, once the laughter died down.

Abby shrugged. "I may've stretched the truth just a bit there," she said with a shrug and a completely non-apologetic smile. "It's hard to prove that someone's tailpipe is the cause of a wildfire, although in this case, the circumstantial evidence *is* pretty compelling. The county prosecutor would've had to agree to press charges against him, and it would've been up to him on whether he thought he could make a good case or not.

The chances are pretty slim that he would've taken it on, although not completely out of the realm of possibilities. But, Billy is always on the hook for one bullshit stunt or another. He'll end up in jail soon for something, I promise. He can't help himself."

Wyatt, who'd been listening to her explanation from his vantage point of the chair at the forms desk, came striding over and pulled his wife against him, laying a big one on her. "It makes me hot when you get all kickass on a guy," he growled when he finally pulled away.

"You guys," Juan protested, clearly mortified that his adopted parents were making out in front of him. "Come onnnn…" Wyatt wrapped his arm possessively around Abby's waist and shot his son a proud grin.

"I think we've learned enough about firefighting for one day," he said to Juan. "Let's go home. Your momma and I need to…uhhh…discuss taxes. In the bedroom. Right away."

Juan patted Sparky one last time – she'd settled down as soon as her previous owner had left – and then pushed himself to a standing position. "I know what you two are doing in there and it ain't taxes," Juan grumbled to himself, following his parents out the door, Maggie Mae on their heels.

"Isn't," Abby corrected him. "I won't have you talking like Billy." The door swung shut behind the Miller family, cutting the rest of the conversation off.

After a few reassuring pets of the head to Sparky, the remaining men went back to training, although Moose only just managed to hang in there by the skin of his teeth. He wanted to go file his own taxes with Georgia. After keeping himself from that very pleasurable activity his whole life, he'd quickly found that it was all he wanted to do. Focusing on almost anything else was becoming harder, not easier, as time went on.

He looked over at Troy who was listening intently as Jaxson walked them through a few simple maneuvers. He'd never been much for talking, but lately, especially since the night of the interview with Penny, he'd come out of his shell a little. Moose wondered if Troy and Penny were also…filing taxes together. Troy was such a private person, Moose wouldn't be surprised if he found out someday that Troy'd married Penny on the sly and just hadn't told anyone.

Marriage…now there was a topic of conversation that'd filled Moose with dread almost his whole life, but which now thrilled him to pieces. Just another couple of months, and he could finally do what he'd been wanting to do since he knew what the words meant.

He was almost there…

CHAPTER 25

GEORGIA

August, 2018

As Georgia pulled a tank top on, Moose mumbled something to the back side of the closet.

"What?" she asked absentmindedly, wiggling into a pair of jean shorts. She looked down at her mostly bare legs, trying to decide if she looked *too* unprofessional on her day off, when Moose pulled his head out of the closet.

"My dad is not..." He trailed off, his eyes raking her from head to toe. "Oh. I..."

His eyes were growing hot with need, and she knew that look. She planted her hands on her hips with a mock glare. "Two times last night and again this morning. You ought to be able to at least finish a sentence."

"Says you," he mumbled. "You're not the one looking at your legs."

She thought about pointing out that she'd spent her whole life looking at her legs, considering they were attached to her, but decided to let it pass. At least for a minute. After all, she didn't exactly mind bringing the cutest guy in three counties to a complete stop just by putting on a pair of jean shorts.

"Your dad is not…?" she prompted.

"Oh. Right." He turned back to the closet, apparently unable to look at her while also talking, and pulled out a pair of tennis shoes. "He isn't going to be happy about the Sawyer Stampede parade today." He sat down in a chair and began pulling them on.

"Why?" Georgia asked suspiciously. She wasn't overly fond of the man, to be sure, but she also wasn't keen on Moose antagonizing him further. They all had to live in the same valley for years to come. There was no reason to make life more miserable than it had to be.

"The float that I'll be in." He looked up and shot her a boyish grin. "I reallllyyyy don't think he's gonna like it."

She arched one eyebrow at him skeptically. "What are you planning, mister? There is no reason your father should hate the Sawyer Fire Department rolling down the street in a fire truck."

"Mister, huh?" he said with a lascivious grin as he stood up and walked over, locking his arms around her lower back and pulling her towards him. "I remember you calling me something quite different a couple of hours ago." His lips started drifting their way down her neck and traitor that her body was, she found herself tilting her head to the side to give him better access.

"That's when you weren't busy pissing off your father," she informed him in her best schoolmarm voice…

Except it came out all breathy and trembly from the need he was stirring up inside of her. Even her voice was traitorous, dammit.

He popped a quick one on her mouth and then let her go; she only barely managed not to fall over from the sudden lack of support. Her legs had gone all rubbery on her. "Just…don't miss my float in the parade, 'kay?" He was serious in that moment, and then it was gone and he was back to grinning at her. "I need to have my best girl there to cheer me on."

"Your *best* girl, huh?" she grumbled, following him to the

front door of their condo. He'd moved in with her not too long after the momentous art and wine tasting in Franklin, swallowing his pride by moving in with her rather than the other way around. After all of the problems that the Garrett male pride had caused, Georgia was damn glad he'd learned to bend a little. "How many other girls do you have?"

"I couldn't tell you that," he said with mock alarm. "Then I couldn't keep you on your toes. See you in a couple of hours on the parade route? You'll sit close to where the announcer is stationed, right?"

"Yeah, sure," she said, and watched his sexy cowboy swagger as he headed to his truck. *Damn*, he was handsome. She'd long ago stopped asking why he wanted the ugly cousin, and just thanked God for the miracle.

She'd planned on going with Tenny to the parade but at the last minute, her cousin said she had to stay home and get some orders done for her new business, so Georgia ended up sitting between Abby Miller and Tripp instead. It was hot in the bright sunshine of August, but Georgia soaked it up like a sponge. Only a few more weeks and they were going to be back to the cold snaps and freezing temps of winter in Idaho. She had to stow the heat away while she could.

"So what float is Moose going to be on?" Abby asked, shading her eyes as she peered down the parade route, waiting for floats to start making an appearance.

"Sawyer Fire Department," Georgia said loudly, trying to make herself heard over the patriotic music piping out of the speakers. Tripp was craning his neck so hard, meanwhile, Georgia was sure a visit to the chiropractor would be in order afterwards. She opened up her mouth to ask him which girl he was drooling over now when Abby spoke again.

"No, he won't."

"No, he won't what?" Georgia repeated absentmindedly, trying to follow the line of sight of Tripp's gaze. He was either drooling over the blonde with more boobs than three women should possess, or the Asian with straight black hair almost to her waist.

Probably both. No reason to only drool over one, right?

Abby tapped her on the arm impatiently. "He won't be with the fire department today. Jaxson was talking about it earlier with Wyatt. No one can get it out of him which float he's going to be on, but the fire truck isn't it."

Georgia's head snapped around and she stared at Abby blankly. "It…it won't?" she stuttered. "He won't? Then what float will he be on?"

Abby rolled her eyes. "Obviously, you are no help." Juan tugged at her arm and she turned to him with a sigh. "Yes?"

"He was driving a big red combine," Juan announced importantly. "Earlier. Over to the start of the parade. The Missy ones."

"Massey Ferguson?" Georgia asked, just wanting to make sure that she was interpreting his comments correctly.

"Yeah, that."

"Oh Lordy," Georgia said under her breath, and then started laughing. "No wonder…"

Abby stared at her, bemused.

"Earlier," Georgia finally said, once she could speak again, "Moose told me that his dad was going to be bent out of shape about the float that he was in. I couldn't figure it out – there was no reason for Rocky to be upset about the fire department truck. Boy howdy though – the oldest son of the owner of the John Deere dealership driving a *Massey Ferguson* combine in the parade? Somebody ought to make sure that Rocky's heart can take this. I hope they have the EMTs on hand, just in case."

The patriotic music broke off suddenly, and Kurtis Workman's voice crackled over the speakers. "Weeelllccccooooommmmmmeeeee to the Sawyer Stampede Parade!" Everyone cheered – even Tripp turned back around in his seat and clapped. The floats began appearing at the bend in the road and inching their way along the route.

"Leading the parade, of course, is this year's Grand Marshall." Kurtis' voice boomed and echoed around them as Georgia watched with polite interest. When particularly generous floats passed in front of them, Juan was quick to snatch up any and all candy, making periodic runs back to Abby to dump handfuls into the sack and then take off again.

"I think the dentist is actually behind all of the parades and parties that we have 'round here," Abby said ruefully to Georgia as Juan dumped yet another load into the pillow sack and then took off at a run. "This sack is filled with ten pounds of sugar. It's a good thing we have a good insurance policy at the county—"

There was an energy rippling through the crowd as every eye on the street turned to look…at Georgia?

Like the crowd's necks had been put on swivels, they all focused on her, and the low rumble of the crowd grew louder by the moment.

"Why is everyone staring at me?" Georgia asked through a tight smile, trying not to move her lips too much. Maybe, this was just a figment of her imagination. Maybe they were staring at Tripp, or at—

"Is *that* Georgia?" she heard a little kid ask in a much-too-loud whisper. She turned to find the child in the crowd pointing straight at her.

Right-o. This was getting stranger by the moment, no doubt about it.

"Here comes Moose and the combine!" Juan hollered with glee as he sprinted over to drop off more of his candy haul. "He's the one driving it and everything."

Juan was right – the combine was about halfway down the block and moving closer by the moment. She would've known it was Moose in the Massey Ferguson combine even if she were blind, though, as whispers of her name flowed through the crowd. More people were turning and even adults were pointing at her now. The cheers were getting raucous as people stomped their feet and yelled, "What's your answer?!"

"What's my answer for *what*?" Georgia hissed under her breath, eyes wide and panicked. She didn't want to admit that she didn't have the faintest idea of what was going on, but if someone didn't clue her in and quick, she was going to have to fess up.

"Oh. Oh my…" Tripp, who was sitting to Georgia's left, was thus just the slightest bit closer to the tractor as it made its way towards them, and with that combined with his height, he was able to spot it first. "Uh, Georgia?"

"Yes??" she whimpered. Did she want to know? She wasn't sure she did.

"I hope you wanna get married."

"You *what*?!" She jerked her head to stare at her second-in-command in aghast. "I am *not* going to marry you." This was, by far, the strangest situation she'd ever been in. Tripp didn't want to marry her. Tripp was her friend and employee. Nothing more than that. He knew she was—

"Not me. God, no. Nothing personal, but I'm not interested." He winked. "Him." He jerked his head at the combine that'd finally made its way close enough that even Georgia could see what it said on the side.

"Up next," Kurtis' voice boomed out, "it looks as if Moose Garrett from the Massey Ferguson dealership has a question for the credit union manager among us. Georgia, what do you say?"

Georgia, will you marry me?

Three-foot-high words hanging off the side of the combine were flapping in the slight breeze as it rolled down the street, but there was no mistaking them. And there was Moose, in the driver's seat, the cab upfront and center, placed so the farmer could have a panoramic view of the field…

Or of the person he was proposing to.

Georgia froze. She couldn't think. She couldn't breathe. She couldn't believe that this was happening to *her*.

"Is he…is he proposing to me?" she whispered, trying not to faint. Perhaps this was all a dream. The most realistic dream of her life.

"Yes," Tripp and Abby whispered back in unison.

She stared blankly ahead, nothing working, no thoughts processing, and then the world swished back into focus as someone jostled into the back of her camp chair, jerking her from suspension.

Moose was proposing. To *her*. This was actually happening, right here, right now.

The massive piece of equipment rolled to a stop directly in front of the announcer's stand…and her. She scrambled to her feet, ignoring the cheers and encouragement from the crowd because she didn't need it now. She knew what she wanted.

She sprinted around the front of the combine to the driver's side, scrambling up the attached ladder and into the cab, a swirl of kisses and happy tears as she threw herself at Moose.

"I'm gonna guess that's a yes, then," the announcer said, and the crowd roared with laughter.

"Are you sure?" Moose whispered, his eyes searching her as he brushed the tears from her cheeks with the pads of his work-hardened thumbs.

"I've never been so sure of anything in my life," Georgia whispered back. "I've loved my cousin's boyfriend my entire life. I never, ever thought he'd love me back."

"Always. You were always the one."

A honk from a float behind them drew them back to the present. "I guess we should probably finish out the parade, eh?" Moose asked with an easy grin. "You can sit in the jump seat and throw candy out the window."

With a reluctant sigh, Georgia moved off Moose's lap and into the jump seat, picking up the bag of candy and making sure to throw an extra large handful straight at Juan. Abby was throwing her kisses, and Tripp was ignoring it all, deep in conversation with a cute girl with mile-long legs.

As they began rolling slowly down the street again, Georgia felt the happy tears make a reappearance. "You, sir, never do anything small, do you?" she said with a laugh as she tossed more candy out the window.

"Now what in the hell would the fun in that be, Georgie?"

As she threw out more candy, she figured, *Not very much fun at all.*

QUICK AUTHOR'S NOTE

HOWDY, y'all! *waving*

I sure hope you enjoyed *Inferno of Love*. The pathway to happily ever after certainly wasn't straight and smooth for Moose and Georgia, but that just makes it all the sweeter in the end.

The spark for *Inferno* (boy, I'm all sorts of punny today!) came straight out of the life of one of my friends. She adopted a gorgeous setter that's white with black spots, after her original owner mistreated the dog and made her gun shy. After the abuse, the dog had a hard time learning to trust again, but she was eventually able to find her forever home with my friend.

Here's a picture of the setter, taking a snooze:

Isn't she just a sweetie?

The first time I saw her setter, I thought it was a Dalmatian, and my friend told me that almost everyone makes that mistake.

Which got me thinking, and when an author gets to thinking…

Well, *Inferno of Love* was the result.

But of course, this is only Book 2 of this series, and the story continues with Book 3. In fact, more than any other book I've ever written, *Inferno* is *highly* intertwined with *Fire and Love* (the love story of Moose's best friend, Levi). Chronologically, *Fire* starts between Chapter 23 and 24 of *Inferno*, right after Moose and Georgia kiss and make-up.

It isn't that you can't read *Fire and Love* as a standalone novel, but…why would you? It's so much better if read *directly* after finishing *Inferno*. (Hint, hint, nudge, nudge).

In *Fire and Love*, you'll find that secrets run deep, but betrayal runs deeper. It is available at your favorite book retailer or local library, so be sure to find it there and enjoy.

Here's to many more years of loving Long Valley together,

Erin Wright

Be sure to find my books at your favorite bookstore, retailer, or library

Or, buy them directly from me at
https://ErinWright.net/My-Books

If you prefer, you can also scan this QR code with your phone:

ALSO BY ERIN WRIGHT

~ COWBOYS OF LONG VALLEY ROMANCE ~

Accounting for Love

Blizzard of Love

Arrested by Love

Returning for Love

Christmas of Love

Overdue for Love

Bundle of Love

Lessons in Love

Baked with Love

Bloom of Love

Broken by Love (TBA)

Holly and Love (TBA)

Banking on Love (TBA)

Sheltered by Love (TBA)

~ FIREFIGHTERS OF LONG VALLEY ROMANCE ~

Flames of Love

Inferno of Love

Fire and Love

Burned by Love

~ MUSICIANS OF LONG VALLEY ROMANCE ~

Strummin' Up Love

Melody of Love (TBA)

Rock 'N Love (TBA)

Rhapsody of Love (TBA)

~ SERVICEMEN OF LONG VALLEY ROMANCE ~

Thankful for Love (TBA)

Commanded to Love (TBA)

Salute to Love (TBA)

Harbored by Love (TBA)

ABOUT ERIN WRIGHT

USA Today Bestselling author Erin Wright has worked every job under the sun, including library director, barista, teacher, website designer, and ranch hand helping brand cattle, before settling into the career she's always dreamed about: Author.

She still loves coffee, doesn't love the smell of cow flesh burning, and is currently living out her own love story in a tiny town in rural Idaho.

Wanna get in touch?
https://erinwright.net
erin@erinwright.net

Or reach out to Erin on your favorite social media platform:

facebook.com/AuthorErinWright

x.com/ErinWrightLV

youtube.com/@ErinWrightLV

pinterest.com/ErinWrightBooks

goodreads.com/ErinWright

bookbub.com/profile/Erin-Wright

instagram.com/AuthorErinWright

9 781950 570836